T0262563

"Unflinching... It's [the] haunting threat of a foreshortened life that sets this work apart from traditional addiction memoirs. Mohr's raw account is equally shocking and moving."
—*Publishers Weekly*

"Joshua Mohr's new memoir, *Model Citizen*, is not for the faint of heart, but there's something profoundly beautiful and deeply humanizing about it, too. The book forces us to reconcile the conflicting truths of our mortal existence—that we are alone in a world that doesn't care about us even a little, even as we're surrounded by and connected to other solitary souls who might just save us if we let them. There's terror here, but comfort, as well."
—**Richard Russo, author of *Chances Are***

"From dozens of perfectly honed scenes combined in a mind and soul satisfying structure, Joshua Mohr has made a book that refuses to look away from all the ugliness, yet makes himself so vulnerable in the telling, that every bit of beauty sticks. Relentlessly honest, hilarious, gut-wrenchingly sad, *Model Citizen* is the opposite of a pull-yourself-up-by-your-bootstraps memoir, and all the more hopeful (and profound) for it."
—**Pam Houston, author of *Deep Creek: Finding Hope In The High Country***

"No one anywhere writes into the gap between grit and grace better than Joshua Mohr. *Model Citizen* dives deep into the crucible of addiction and recovery and then breathes life back into us all. How thrilling to encounter a story in which I can feel both named as well as loved alongside a narrator who I respect and admire for diving down into the depths and bringing something back for the rest of us. A ride or die book. This book changed my life."
—**Lidia Yuknavitch, author of *Verge***

## PRAISE FOR *TERMITE PARADE*

"[A] wry and unnerving story of bad love gone rotten. [Mohr] has a generous understanding of his characters, whom he describes with an intelligence and sensitivity that pulls you in. This is no small achievement."
—*The New York Times Book Review* (**Editor's Choice**)

Similar to Dostoyevsky's *Crime and Punishment*: the most crucial action serves as a portal to and wellspring for the various psychologies of its characters. But Mohr's storytelling is so absorbing that *Termite Parade* does not read like an analytical rumination; if he is examining the very nature of these characters under a microscope, he at least lets the specimens speak for themselves."
—*San Francisco Chronicle*

"*Termite Parade* is a sucker punch to literary complacency, without a hint of authorial self-absorption. Mohr is a post-millennial Bukowski with a dash of Hubert Selby, Jr. thrown in for good measure, and with only two published novels under his belt, he is rapidly becoming one of my favorite American novelists."
—*Powell's Review-A-Day*

## PRAISE FOR *DAMASCUS*

"*Damascus* succeeds in conveying a big-hearted vision."
—*The Wall Street Journal*

"At once gripping, lucid and fierce, *Damascus* is the mature effort of an artist devoted to personal growth and as such contains the glints of real gold."
—*San Francisco Chronicle*

# SAINT THE TERRIFYING

## A VIKING PUNK SAGA: VOLUME 1

## JOSHUA MOHR

THE UNNAMED PRESS
LOS ANGELES, CA

*For those of us with tall tales in our tall hearts*

# SAINT THE TERRIFYING

# PART 1

## THESE ARE THE LIGHTS
## THAT TAKE US AWAY

# 1

YOU'RE A PERSON who has this story forming in your mind's eye, that marvelous imagination, that wonder hunter, that thunderstorm, that haunted house filled with the fertilizer of childhood, that drive-in showing dirty movies, that therapist's couch, that dive bar, that frantic machine, that solitary confinement, that butcher cleaving your memories to meat, that manic depressive, that flat saxophone, that anxious child, that father's gnarled love, that mother's cusses and knuckles hustling around your skull, punishing, still punishing, and why can't we ever shush the roars from our—

Wait.

What were we talking about?

Yeah. Right. The day I "killed" Got Jokes.

Someone did die that day, but unfortunately, it wasn't him.

If that sounds mean, it's only because you don't know Got Jokes yet.

Look, it was supposed to be their big break, the best night of their lives. I know that because he said so. I was the guy you talked to when things went sideways. Maybe it was the NO MORE DRUNKEN MADNESS tattoo on my neck—or it was the look in my blue eye versus the fake one. Lost its predecessor when a blade lanced through, like it was an olive on a cocktail stick, and now I wore a scrubs-blue replacement that always seemed surprised, too wide.

I played guitar in a crappy band called Slummy. We had no future. But I wished you could have seen how happy it made us to pollute the world with those broken songs.

Got Jokes played in a great band next door at Sound Check, our rehearsal space. There were forty bands who rented rooms. When you were here at night, and we all wailed through amplifiers at the same time, it sounded like the jungle. The studio was close to 880, and that freeway groused and squealed and screeched with speeding tires. These cars wanted everyone to know that their engines were hearts, and those hearts were filled with gasoline.

Got Jokes was their guitarist. Trick Wilma sang and played bass in All the Fuss. She wrote true and angry songs; she was the real deal. They were a couple, and when Got Jokes put his guitar parts to her music, it suddenly sounded like Green Day had their period.

So, basically, Green Day.

ᚹ

I'd lived in West Oakland since it was *really* West Oakland. Smash and grabs were cross streets. The whole neighborhood got pistol-whipped, spitting teeth. It was so deranged that people even took runs at me. I did righteous violence. Berserker beatings. But my hands got carried away one night. There should've been voices shouting in my head to stop, and maybe there were. Maybe I just couldn't hear them, drowning in the liquor gurgling in my brain. And if I couldn't hear them, I couldn't hear his skull fracture on that fender.

I did eighteen months in county, eight years at Quentin. Got my fake eye in there. My good luck charm. Really. My life had gotten better since popping in that always-surprised fake.

I was tattooed in there, too. Got my NO MORE DRUNKEN MADNESS. The script looked god-awful, but to me, it was the Declaration of Independence.

Those Quentin cages, no, I wanted more sky, wanted to breathe the air after a spring rain, wanted to bungee, to surf, to lie in the sun so long my skin pulsed, wanted to drink a glass of too-sour lemonade, eat a churro as long as an elephant's trunk. I wanted to lick pussy for an hour straight, steal a motorcycle and ride to Stinson Beach at eighty.

I returned from lockup clean, better; after a year in a halfway house, I made it back to West Oakland—and it had a Whole Foods.

Þ

I lived in a punk house. The cover story was that it was a twenty-four-hour artists' space, wasn't zoned to be residential, slapped in between an industrial laundromat and shoe manufacturer—but we lived here, oh yes, we loved it here, oh yes, our zoo, our mental hospital, our bus station, and I awoke every day ecstatic to live in this vulgar empire, and I always hitched to the studio as soon as my feet hit the floor, couldn't wait for my hands to revive my guitar, but we aren't supposed to be talking about music, not yet, no, now, I was telling you about the punk house and how it ran on exhausted wiring, a vascular system of fraying cords snaking through the whole building, which was one immense, open floor that we divvied up by square feet, made our own art cages, made a hallway-maze of old pianos down its center, the whole room was its own project really, constantly being added to, tweaked, remixed, right now a wheelbarrow with a stalk of corn growing in it, a mural of old picture frames on a brick wall, a crow's nest, bicycles everywhere, a sculpture of a cherry tree, a small sailboat, chandeliers hanging from knotted and tangled wires, old computers stacked in the shape of a crucifix with a papier-mâché Steve Jobs nailed on top, an RV, a grow room, a Subaru Outback with its engine compartment used as a closet, mannequins, tents, loft beds, bunk beds, hammocks, futons; we were welders, record store workers, socialists, bipolar baristas, neurodivergence enthusiasts, sullen photographers, construction crews running on amphetamines, artists of every variety—we even had a med school dropout who treated our infected wounds, cats, dogs, birds, a potbelly pig, an iguana named Danzig—the occasional child running around, barefoot and scrawny and hobo feral at three, tarot readers, telepaths, astrologists, bartenders, masseuses, spoken word philosophers, performance artists, sex workers, actors, acrobats, poets, pole dancers, comedians, runaways, junkies, buskers, junkie buskers, survivors, crooks; we had an MMA gym, a not-quite-legal tattoo and piercing shop, a cheap recording studio, and musicians and musicians and musicians, amplifiers, drums, next to litter boxes, kiddie pools, easels, a pasta cooker, laundry lines, pots catching drips, indoor plants of diverse origins—some living, some left to self-compost—fictitious taxidermy animals nailed to wooden walls next to rock and roll flyers, Tibetan flags, a red right hand, missing children posters, a Black Flag logo, a PJ Harvey still from a festival gig, a photorealist portrait of Trotsky on a huge stretched canvas, thirty by thirty—and we built a second story, rickety as it was, we duct-taped and finger fucked it, we made it ourselves, goddamn it, and we were proud that we worked so hard on it and threw events up there, concerts, both bands and DJs, fashion shows, plays, readings, all kinds of dance, even had a schizophrenic play the didgeridoo once, lying flat on his back, balancing the ten-foot trunk of the instrument from his open mouth, never using his arms once to steady it, swaying delicately, and he controlled his breathing, slowly, sounding like an opiate buzz, in and out, blowing his blue tune through that chimney, and we watched him do this for an hour straight, unbelievably transfixed—

And that concludes my punk house description that sounds like a punk song.

You could clap now if you saw fit.

ᚦ

Inside Sound Check, I ate a Pop-Tart and changed the strings on my Tele when Got Jokes started pounding on my practice room's door. It was good timing for company, as I'd just pasted my mohawk into liberty spikes.

Remember, it was supposed to be the night of his band's big break. All the Fuss got a last-minute supporting slot on the evening's Jawbreaker bill at 924 Gilman Street, which was the only club any of us cared about playing. Our wrecked Mecca. Our Graceland with scabies. It would be the first time their band played to a packed house.

"What do you want?" I yelled on my way to the door, not yet knowing it was him. (I wasn't a morning person.)

Once I saw him there, I broke the Pop-Tart in half and handed him his fifty. I liked Got Jokes okay, back then.

"Gear's all gone!" he shouted at me.

He was the handsome one in their band, and I resented him for it. My false blue eye scared most women the same way it scared most men.

"Slow down," I said. "Who took the gear where?"

"Jesse stole it."

That was their junkie manager—and this was how every story about every junkie manager who ever stole from punk rockers ended. The musicians, empty-handed. The manager, comatose and pleased.

"What are you going to do?" I said.

"How should I know? That's why, like, I'm here. I'm asking you, man. You gotta fucking help me."

I wasn't going to get upset that he swore at me. I was working on my temper. There were days when I bordered on nice. I had given him half the Pop-Tart, which was above and beyond the call—and somehow remained an uneaten, enraging prop in his hand.

I hated these moments, seeing this new sensitivity blooming in me. Was I really concerned with the rate that another man gobbled his breakfast? I was getting soft, gentrified like West Oakland. Maybe I had a Whole Foods, too.

"He even took the power strips," he said.

We glared at each other.

"Try the goddamn Pop-Tart," I said.

"The what?"

I pointed at the pastry in his hand.

He looked at it. "Oh yeah."

"Frosted cherry," I said. "Your favorite."

"That's not my favorite."

"It should be."

He thoughtlessly nibbled, then put most of it in his pocket. It bothered me how quickly he talked again. Why wouldn't he want to savor the poetry of that breakfast dessert? But Got Jokes went right on: "I don't know how to find anybody. Do you? Can you help?"

"Depends."

"On what?"

"Can you say thank you for the fucking Pop-Tart?" I asked.

Þ

You're a person who has this hazy understanding of me, ingesting various traits line by line, bite by bite, bringing me into your system, sifting through the food of these ideas, harvesting nutrients, that truth, that nourishment, the way we gorge ourselves on Story to feel something. I took writing classes at Quentin, teachers coming through—which usually meant sticking around for a session or three till they realized that we had pencils and they had throats—but I fell in love with escaping into stories, that was what we junkies did anyway, disappearing into squalid museums that only we could see, animating the dead, talking to fraudulent gods, soaring with pterodactyls, dancing with handsome criminals, lounging in whirlpools with angels who had the lax breasts of mothers—

Wait.

What were we talking about?

Yeah. Okay. Got Jokes.

He finally said thanks for the Pop-Tart, so I agreed to help him hunt down Jesse. It wasn't like you needed to call in the bloodhounds to find a junkie. There were only three options: he was on the run with the gear, or he was trying to hock it all on the quick, or he had the sale set up ahead of time and was already holed up in a motel shooting drugs.

The cops wouldn't care about the Jawbreaker gig, wouldn't care that, to us punks, playing that kind of show was making it. We weren't greedy. All we wanted was a room full of sweaty pals crashing into one another, having the time of their lives. We wanted one kid to come up after and say, "You! Rock!"

A dime bag of ramen and a forty of Olde E, and we were good. That was all the success we were ever going to know.

Except for Green Day.

But fuck them.

"Where are we going first?" Got Jokes asked me. He was pulling his crappy maroon Reliant that must've been made in 1956 out of Sound Check's parking lot. I didn't own a car. I walked miles around Oakland and Berkeley. I rode BART. Took the bus. I was crazy enough to hitchhike, assuming you were crazy enough to pick me up.

From the stereo, the singer of Fang invited us to his suicide.

The day gave off a gray stare. You never knew if the fog was gonna burn off, not that I cared. It gave me an excuse to wear sunglasses before noon.

Got Jokes swigged out of a flask. Bourbon. Old Crow.

The smell of his liquor made me salivate, made my good eye go surprised, too.

"I have an idea," I said.

"Whatever it is," he said, "I'm on board. You're the brains behind this operation."

Nobody had ever called me the brains before, and I imagined this was what it must feel like if your parents ever gave you a compliment. Mine were fonder of dying young.

"It will sound kinda mad," I said.

"Stop qualifying," he said. "I'm all ears!"

"Let's go break into his house," I said.

Got Jokes went from all ears to all wide eyes, staring at me and not the road that wound through a maze of empty industrial buildings. "I definitely can't play the gig tonight if we get arrested," said Got Jokes.

"Look at the road," I said.

"The what?"

"The thing we're driving on."

"Right," he said. "That." And his gaze returned to the pavement beyond the windshield.

"Do you want clues or not?" I asked.

"But he could be there."

I knew Jesse wouldn't be there. What, you stole the gear and then went to take a bubble bath, make a quesadilla? He was a hundred miles away by now.

"No way he's there," I said.

It felt good to be needed. Got Jokes came to me, and that made it easier to excuse the flask. He didn't know how hard I was working to stay clean.

He only knew I was a Viking.

ᚠ

Ten minutes later, we pulled up to Jesse's apartment building, the three of us: Got Jokes, me, and the flask. The entire block was made up of 1970s apartment buildings, stucco palaces.

"Have you ever broken into a house before?" I asked him. My one real eye glared.

"We can't commit a crime, man," said Got Jokes. "We're, like, trying to solve one."

"And how can we do that if we don't get some clues?"

"I see what you mean," he said, "but I'm too pretty for prison."

He was right about that. "I'll do it, Captain Pretty. Sit here, suckle your flask, and I'll be right back."

I wasn't too worried. This was a *mind your business* building, one that would no doubt soon be razed. Replaced with a gleaming set of those trophy case condos. Restaurants made out of glass on the ground floor.

Gyms with windows like OnlyFans channels, so passersby could peep inside and see all the titillating self-improvement. But for now, this crappy place was filled with a collection of disasters who insisted on being left alone in their particular tentacles of suffering. So I didn't need to worry about making noise at Jesse's because of the neighbors. I'd kick the door down.

Remember, this wasn't a crime. This was me doing the right thing.

Unhinged?

Un-no.

This was gonna be a virtuous door-kicking-in.

An avenging angel didn't need permission to save the day.

It didn't get more hinged than that.

ᚦ

You're a person at a run-down apartment, at his drab headquarters, his home base, his home planet, his bunker, his hideout, his crater of junk-iedom, his cavity search, his stop-and-frisk, his field sobriety test, his pit of botched assurances, his grimy church, where he betrayed, where he smoked every oath he made Got Jokes and the band, where he put his habit above all else, puking up promises, commitments, and once we burn our honor, life was just a circle pit filled with skeletons that—

Wait.

Where were we?

Yeah. Right. Crashing into Jesse's.

His unit was on the second floor. I stomped up the stairs toward his place, ready for thunder, to kick in the door—but it was open. I could hear somebody singing the blues over an acoustic guitar, no other instruments. Just a man spilling his charred guts. I stayed at the door for a few seconds, listening. It was an old Robert Johnson song, "When You Got a Good Friend."

And so I went inside.

The record player and speakers were in the corner, on the floor. From across the empty room, I could see the needle had fluff on it, the song sounding half submerged, skipping some, making Johnson stutter. There was only one window, mostly blocked with a twin mattress. The kitchen was empty as well. Then I heard water splashing from the bathroom.

I walked slowly toward it, and the Vikings who lived in my bloodstream got ready for the battlefield. The door was closed. There were stickers all over its outside, the same circular sticker, at least twenty of them: WARNING! THIS PRODUCT MIGHT CONTAIN TREE NUTS.

I'd felt disappointed that I didn't get to kick in his front door, so this one would have to do.

A leg raised.

A motivated boot.

A smile on my face.

The whole door flying from its perch and landing on the floor.

Jesse actually *was* taking a bath!

He wasn't alone, lying in the tub. There were five or six pancakes with him, floating on top of the water like lily pads. There were no bubbles. He lay there naked, so emaciated that all his tattoos looked like they'd been done right on his bones. He had a black-and-white Superman *S* running across his whole chest, which seemed the equivalent of nicknaming a tall guy Tiny.

"Where's their gear?" I said, ready for his excuse. We could rationalize anything—file facts down to what we needed them to be, like making shivs in prison.

He smiled, picked up one of the lily pads: "This is my last supper."

"I'm pagan—and it's barely noon."

"I adore pancakes. They seem . . . supportive. Want one?"

"I'm a Pop-Tart man myself."

He let the lily-cake plop back in the bathwater. "I can't bring myself," he said, "to eat these friendly flapjacks."

"Their gear. Now."

He held up a razor blade that had been on the tub's edge and said to me, "I asked this razor a minute ago if there was a reason to reconsider. Then you walked in. Are you here to save me?" He stuck his arm out of the tub, dripping water on the linoleum and the unhinged door. He turned his palm toward the ceiling, traced a vein with the blade. "I've always wanted to see where we go."

It would've been so easy: bang his forearm on the bathtub, knock the razor loose—though of course the compound fracture might have been less pleasant. But that wasn't me anymore, or I didn't want it to be. I waited for him to answer my question.

"I didn't take their gear," he said. "I only unlocked the door for them."

"Them?"

"It wasn't even enough to cover my debt. They're going to kill me tomorrow, so I'm going to kill me today."

You needed to be in this bathroom to understand how broken he was. I'd been that broken. I'd been him. Drugs squeezed the human out of you, leaving only a suicidal amoeba.

The raging Vikings quieted in me, and this moment was no longer about the band's gear; it was about empathy. The world hated junkies, wishing us to the great garbage dump in the sky. Maybe that was where he was going to end up anyway, but that didn't mean he couldn't glimpse a speck of kindness right now.

I plucked my fake eye from the socket, held it out to him. "This is a pill," I said. "It made my life better. It can help you, too. Eat it—and I swear, it will end all those aches in your heart."

Jesse looked at the eye like it was poison. And maybe it was. I had no idea what it would feel like to try to pass a fake eye. But those were issues for later. This was all about now, helping him mute the voice from the razor blade that wanted him dead.

"It will help me?" he asked.

"You'll be . . . like me . . . free now."

Jesse opened his mouth, shut his eyes, waiting for me to give him the filthy Communion. I held my fake, surprised eye up near my face one last time. I stared at myself. Sometimes you needed to lose half your sight to see twice as much. And so I thanked the eye for the fortunes it brought. I didn't mean money. I'd never be rich, but it made my life better by showing me every day that there wasn't a thing that couldn't be bent back into some semblance of shape, even people.

And I'd never forget that eye.

And Jesse would never understand that I got my eye after sobering up in county—and how, from there, slowly, violently, my life got better. I wasn't greedy. I was happy to share this secret for a better life with him. Why? Because his loneliness was louder than that Robert Johnson record, and his loneliness was wetter than that bath, and his loneliness lay off its hinges on the floor. And that razor blade was just a way to ask why you were given a life starved of love. That eye brought me back, and I was going to do the same for Jesse. Show him that there could be a future if he kicked.

I plopped it on his tongue, and he used a handful of pancake crumbs and bathwater to wash me down.

He kept his eyes closed but now smiled.

I waited a beat before I told him I wanted to take him somewhere.

"I can't walk," said Jesse. "I've been boneless all morning."

I picked him out of the tub, slid a ratty towel around his waist, ready to carry him to the car.

"I need to show you something," I said.

ᚦ

You're a person and I'm a person, and she is and he is, and everyone's a person, and Got Jokes is a person who wanted to get pissed seeing me deposit Jesse in the back seat of his crappy maroon Reliant, but he couldn't because he was scared of me, and I finally remembered what we were meant to be talking about this whole time: joy.

Because we were alive—and we could be whoever we wanted. I hopped into the passenger seat, elated, like I'd just survived a near-death experience. And I had. It just wasn't mine.

"Where the hell's your eye?" asked Got Jokes.

"Don't worry about me," I said. "I'm great."

"So why's this prick here?"

I didn't appreciate his tone. He talked to people like they worked for him. "When are you planning on saying thanks?" I asked him.

"Right after you tell me why this prick's here. Does he have our gear?"

"No."

"So who does?"

"I don't know yet. But Jesse will tell me."

Got Jokes mean-mugged Jesse in the rearview: "Where's our gear, asshole?"

"He'll tell me," I said, "not you."

"Why?"

"Because I gave him my eye."

"Oh, right. That makes perfect sense."

"He needs to see something," I said, "and the only way I can show it to him is if we go together."

"You want to give him a ride?!"

"I am giving him a ride."

"He stole our stuff! We should be giving him a ride to jail."

I got out and walked around the Reliant, opened the driver's-side door: "I'll drive."

And I did, after Got Jokes slid into the passenger seat.

I tried to cheer him up by saying, "You can borrow our gear for your gig tonight. You'll still have your big break."

"I appreciate that. But does he really have to come with us?"

ᛈ

I took us to where we needed to go. We idled in the parking lot, looking at the big building.

"Why are we here?" Got Jokes asked.

"Did you ever eat that Pop-Tart?" I asked in answer.

"I must've left it at the studio."

"It's in your pocket."

"Oh, right." He pulled it out. It was in his hand, looking at me, right in my one eye, even more offensive than the flask.

Frosted cherry. My favorite.

"Jesse's a thief," said Got Jokes.

"He should go to prison," said Got Jokes.

"He's a piece of shit," said Got Jokes.

Then he turned around and threw the Pop-Tart at Jesse in the back seat. It hit him right in his Superman tattoo and fell on the towel wrapped around his waist.

I told you earlier that I wasn't a morning person; I was also not an afternoon person. I grabbed Got Jokes's hand that had held the Pop-Tart and I twisted it, and I bent it, and I broke it. He hunched up against the door of the car and started screaming: "The gig! I can't play! You killed me, man! It's over!"

I got out of the car and helped Jesse cinch that towel again.

"How does his half of the Pop-Tart sound?" I asked Jesse.

"I'll try," he said, "but your eye sorta filled me up."

I gave him the Pop-Tart and he took a bite, said, "Thanks."

"Are you still feeling boneless?" I asked him.

He nodded.

I did the thing he needed most: I picked him up again.

"Why did you hurt me?" Got Jokes yelled.

It wasn't the time to get into it, but if he asked later, I'd tell him the truth: Big breaks, like their Jawbreaker gig, were nice, but Jesse needed something more important, a little break. He needed to know that another human could show compassion.

"Just wait here," I said to Got Jokes.

I carried Jesse toward the big building.

"Where are we going?" he asked.

"We're going inside," I said.

And I carried him all the way into West Oakland's Whole Foods, into those bright lights. A room that smelled of cedar. Carting Jesse and his towel into this Valhalla was the happiest I'd been in a long time.

"I like it in here," I said to Jesse, holding him steady, holding him high. "What do you think?"

And just because the gods dug screwing with us, it finally registered for me who was singing over the store's speakers.

Goddamn Green Day.

# 2

WAY I FIGURED IT, I had one day to save Jesse's life—and I was going to do just that.

He said somebody was going to kill him tomorrow.

To that I said, *Well, we'll see.*

I knew where the day had to go now, and that meant calling Dusty. He played bass in Slummy and had always been rock solid when shit slid sideways. A true friend. Loyal. Resourceful. And nothing proved his, shall we say, unique brand of resourcefulness more than his job, the one he invented.

Dusty drove a cab and sold cocaine. You actually copped in the cab. If you were in the know, you called up, and he chauffeured you away, speeding around the neighborhood, while you were in the back trying to steer a key of coke to your nose.

In addition to the band, we worked together. Okay, technically, I worked for him. He'd asked me to muscle in his cab, never squawked any of that boss talk. So he'd drive and I'd sit shotgun with a foot of lead pipe on my lap. Dusty also had a mustache, which he called his "dustache," which meant that he was cooler than all of us.

Dusty always high-piloted the rowdy cab, doing more drugs than he sold. He even sang, "There's dandruff in my dustache!" to the tune of "We Wish You a Merry Christmas," when he spilled powder on his face. I didn't understand how he stayed in business, but he paid me well under the table—and I'd had to put the lead pipe, my "hitter-quitter," to work only a few times.

And before you get a gust of the ol' high and mighty about Dusty being a bad influence on me, he didn't drink. I could be around people on cocaine because it was never my drug. I'd had it only once—a single six-inch line—too much for my first foray, but I didn't know—and I inhaled that sad magic, and suddenly I looked down at my hand, and, huh, it held a telescope, one that showed the future, and, huh, I pointed it at the horizon and gazed intently into it and saw these appalling and coming-to-boil traumas—the earth was too hot and water was another endangered species and civilizations smeared to history and slander, computers were overbearing fathers who served capital punishment at the dinner table, and the mother we hadn't seen in fifteen years stormed back into the house with a can of gas and a look in her eyes that could start the fire itself—but the fire wasn't a real fire, not one that burned you up completely, no, this was some kind of semi-fire, one that set you ablaze, yes, but it didn't cook or kill you, no, didn't even hurt, you went about your dumb day, living your life on fire—

Then the gak wore off. That was enough for me.

I called Dusty after getting kicked out of Whole Foods. Turned out they weren't keen on Jesse wearing only a towel. Dusty had trouble understanding why I dug being in some tragic Whole Foods in the first place, but it was hard to describe. I had no love for forty-dollar rolls of hand-stitched toilet paper, but since getting clean, I had a Whole Foods in me, too. A part of me wanted a relaxed life, but that impulse couldn't win a fight with the punk rockers and Vikings in me.

Jesse had the feral heart of an addict, but we didn't have to ache that way. We could civilize our hearts. Find calm. Find peace. Learn how to love *quiet*. I wanted to carry Jesse inside of all that.

Dusty met us at Got Jokes's Reliant in the grocery store's parking lot. I got a waft of the West Oakland funk. This place had a wastewater treatment plant. It was all rotten eggs, and it hit around the clock. Boggy. Mangy tang. One of the bands who practiced at Sound Check called West Oakland "the world's greatest litter box." A term of endearment. We loved it here, rotten eggs and all. It was our home.

Dusty pointed at Got Jokes. "Why's he here?" They knew each other from Sound Check's halls, vending machines, and crooked ping-pong table.

"We'll get to him in a minute," I said to Dusty, then I nodded toward Jesse, who was curled up resting on the Reliant's hood in his towel. "He's my new friend, and he needs our help."

"Okay—but let's get back to the douche. Why's Got Jokes here?" Dusty asked.

"Dust, I can hear you, man," said Got Jokes.

"I broke his hand," I said to Dusty.

"I'm sure he deserved it."

"He did not!" said Got Jokes.

"Will you help him get it fixed," I said to Dusty, "and take him home?"

"He ruined my life," Got Jokes said to Dusty. "My old lady's going to kill me. He ruined her life, too."

"What's he talking about?" Dusty said to me.

"They got the Jawbreaker supporting slot tonight."

"Oh, nice," said Dusty. "I mean: Oh, shit."

"Trick's gonna flip." Then Got Jokes looked at me: "Oh, shit, what should I tell her?"

"Tell her the truth," I said, "or lie. I don't care. Listen, I'm borrowing your car, Got Jokes. And before you say anything else stupid, listen again: I'm sorry I broke your hand. I shouldn't have done that. So now I'm going to do something nice for you. I'm going to get your gear back today."

"I don't need the gear," Got Jokes said, "I need my fucking hand."

"You need both," I said.

"Anything else?" Dusty asked me.

"Thanks for showing up," I said to him, tucking Got Jokes into the back of the cab. I snatched the hitter-quitter and slid it in the back of my jeans, under my shirt. "I owe you one."

"Go easy," Dusty said, and I said, "I'll go as they make me."

They drove off, and I only half believed Dusty would take him to get his mitt fixed. But the odds were better with him than if Got Jokes had stuck with us. He had too much Green Day in him for me.

I got Jesse stowed in the car. I turned the music up. It was still Fang shrieking their music, and now, the singer told us that he was going to Hollywood. But he was telling lies. That singer ended up doing six years for murdering his girlfriend.

I put my seat belt on, slid the Reliant, which must've been made in 1931, into drive. My foot barely tapped the accelerator before I said to Jesse, "Okay, tell me everything about these guys who are gonna kill you."

"Do you know that psycho Wes Than Zero?" he asked me.

Þ

**From:** Wesley Z <wes.than.zero@gmail.com>
**To:** Toby O'Rourke <Toby@stinkphinger.com>
**Sent:** Wednesday, November 25, 2015 3:43 AM
**Subject:** The Future of Rock & Roll

Some say that rock and roll is a wheezing grandma, weakly rapping on death's door, but don't tell that to the Trauma Bottoms, the Bay Area's newest heavy metal studs. They're here to shove some guitar-induced truth down the naysayers' throats. They'll blotch the world in lamb's blood and catapult the crowd down an express elevator to Hades.

You can quote me on that, Toby.

Lead guitarist Joshy Deathwish writes all their soon-to-be boocoo hits, and you might recognize his name from fronting local legends the Slobbering Dongs. Joshy is that perfect combination of songwriter and sensitive lyricist, and the young man is easy on the eyes. Let the creaming commence!

And the creaming won't simply be south of the border, my man. There will be ear-creaming for both women and men alike. Once the kids get a chance to hear the Trauma Bottoms' spellbinding sound, before you know it, the wheezing grandma that is rock and roll, well, she's going to pop up off that gurney. She'll peel off her top, shake her ta-tas . . .

Toby, we are reaching out to you and only you. Why? Well, you are the gatekeeper, mi amigo. You hold all the power. You singlehandedly have the authority to give the Trauma Bottoms their first big break.

We are regulars at Stink Phinger. Anybody who's anybody knows that your joint is where young rock and roll cubs go to turn into rock and roll lions. Me and the band were at Stink Phinger last Wednesday and had the privilege of seeing the Half-Pint Gigolos
cover Black Sabbath songs. Stature be damned, those dwarfs have hearts the size of wrecking balls. Little men, mighty sound.

One last thing and I'll leave you to listen to the guys shred. You're probably asking yourself: Why the hell is this guy called Wes Than Zero even sending me a CD in 2015? What obsolete technology will Wes send me next—a landline, a cassette, asthma inhalers filled with asbestos?

Toby, when you remove the CD from the case, you'll notice a bindle behind it. You'll notice that it is filled with powder. You might snort it and see what happens.

You know what they say, my man: If you're going to stoop to bribery, it better be cocaine.

Wes Than Zero

Þ

**From:** Wesley Z <wes.than.zero@gmail.com>
**To:** Toby O'Rourke <Toby@stinkphinger.com>
**Sent:** Thursday, November 26, 2015 4:06 AM
**Subject:** Carrot or Stick?

Ahoy, capitan! Que onda? This is your new friend, Wes Than Zero, the generous man who yesterday gave you a couple of presents. First, that was good shit, yeah? You probably couldn't feel your face all day after that bump. You can say you're welcome by booking these guys a gig, because they are the second gift I gave you.

Listen, between me and you, I know I laid it on a little thick about the Trauma Bottoms. Fine. You got me. Maybe you listened to the CD and thought, *This is the band he's touting as the future of rock and roll?* Hey, I boocoo know they're not Bowie or Black Flag.

But I also know your real name.

I know where you live.

I've been on your houseboat.

I know there is Tupperware filled with spaghetti with meat sauce on the second shelf of your fridge.

So now's when you shut up and book the band.

I live in the wind, so if you do the wrong thing here and call the cops, I'll get to you before the police get to me. So do the easy thing. It's one gig. Book it. And I'm out of your hair.

Carrot or stick?

Wes Than Zero

ᚦ

**From:** Wesley Z <wes.than.zero@gmail.com>
**To:** Toby O'Rourke <Toby@stinkphinger.com>
**Sent:** Friday, November 27, 2015 12:11 PM
**Subject:** Good Boy

I'm feeling relief, Toby! Thank you. I'm thrilled that you've decided to come on board the houseboat of our new friendship and do the right thing. It only makes sense. We've stumbled upon a mutually beneficial situation. It's wonderful when we all end up on top. We're a couple of number one hits, huh?

The sky's the limit, muchacho. We make a good team.

And maybe that's the problem—us being such a boocoo good team. How can being *good* be bad? Because we're too good! And why stop at one, let's be honest, crap band and one measly little gig?

I say we carpe diem the bejeezus out of this bitch. Here's what we'll do: I'll periodically send you new CDs—always with an on-the-house extra tucked behind the disc—and you agree to book that band for a show. One show! No biggie! In fact, I'm really doing your job for you, gift-wrapping these bands, and that's yet another benefit from this for you. Wow, you're sure coming out on top in our partnership!

It's going to be such a simple relationship, once all this cockroach bureaucracy is sorted out between us, once I know that we're on the same page and can trust each other. Then it's all about the music. That's why we got into this business in the first place, right?

You do this and I'll never board your houseboat again. I'll forget about that Tupperware'd spaghetti with meat sauce.

Let's have some fun.

Wes Than Zero

ᚦ

That was the con's launch, a year or so back—and once Wes had this booker in his back pocket, the rest took care of itself. He trolled for new and naive bands, set them up with "managers" like Jesse, secured them that precious first gig.

Once they had the show booked, the managers convinced the bands that their gear wasn't good enough. Scrape together whatever loot they could, buy top of the line. The managers said things like "If this is your dream, go all in."

And most of them did. You couldn't blame them: This dream had been squatting in their bodies since puberty, and someone came along and told them exactly what they wanted to hear. They didn't even need to be hustled, not really. They'd already been hustled by their dreams.

Once they'd spent all their money on gear, that was when the manager would leave the rehearsal space's door open—and the band got cleaned out by Wes's crew. They'd pulled this hustle, said Jesse, on about twenty bands. They'd pulled in a little over a hundred grand so far. Wes had a handful of people like Jesse, people who would do anything to stay high. People so mangled on heroin that they'd steal a band's gear.

Jesse was crying when he told me all this. But you couldn't trust a crying junkie. There was an old joke that illustrated this: What was the difference between a drunk and a junkie?

An alcoholic might steal your money one night, but he or she would show up the next day, sobbing and making amends. They'd want a hug. You'd have to give the whole *there, there* schtick, and the drunkard would promise to pay you back, insincerely, no doubt.

A junkie, however, would steal your wallet, and the next morning, he or she would show up at your place and help you look for it, feigning surprise when the two of you couldn't track it down. *Huh, this is the strangest thing!* the helpful junkie might say. *Where on earth could it be?*

I looked over at Jesse. Maybe I should have told the joke to him as a distraction. He was coming down, his high abandoning him. He'd need some sugar maintenance soon.

"We'll go to Stink Phinger and talk to this booker," I said, "but I need to pick up something on our way."

ᛈ

I was missing my eye. I didn't mind giving it to Jesse. He needed it more than me. But I didn't want to have an empty socket, some cave in my face, some defect. I already felt that people didn't like looking my way. So we pulled into a strip mall and parked right in front of the army supply store. There were no other cars in the lot, and each of the other five storefronts had FOR LEASE signs.

I left Jesse dozing in the ride, and the bell tinkled as I came in. The store was empty, save for the woman working. She was back behind the counter, and her eyes were red, bloodshot, and her whole face was irritated in a sickening rash. She looked pale, shaken; there was snot on her lip. She wheezed, coughed, but in some demented *the show must go on* way, she welcomed me into the shop with the enthusiasm of a cruise ship captain, crooning, "Please make yourself at home!"

Wheezing, coughing.

"Are you okay?" I asked.

"Oh, don't mind me. I pepper sprayed myself—accidentally. One of those days." She smiled, which made it worse, her poisoned face pretending that this was a normal thing. "I'm Hild."

"Did you rinse out your eyes yet?" I said.

"I was gonna."

"When?"

"When they start working again. I can't even see you, baby." Hild was pushing seventy, hair dyed redder than her freaking-out face.

"I knew you couldn't see me," I said, "because I'm a foot to the left of where you're staring."

She repositioned to "look" straight at me.

"How'd I do this time?" she asked.

Wheezing, coughing.

"You nailed it," I said.

"You're my first customer of the day. What can I help you with?"

"I also have an eye issue."

"Pepper spray?"

"I wish. Do you sell eye patches?"

Then she started crying. Really crying. "These are happy tears," Hild said.

They didn't seem like happy ones. She was inconsolable. I watched for fifteen, twenty seconds. She cried like she was alone, like I wasn't even there. She cried like a polar bear surrounded by melting ice, cried like a soldier who saw a set of legs lying a few feet away that looked familiar, cried like a tree being cut down for condos.

"Really, those are happy tears?" I asked. "You look super upset."

"I was feeling sorry for myself, with the pepper spray and all. But here you are, showing me that it isn't that big of a deal. At least I got two eyes."

"I can lead you to the bathroom," I said. "We can clean your eyes."

"It's in the back."

I walked behind the counter, placed Hild's hand on my shoulder, and slowly led her.

"Someone sent you here to cheer me up," she said.

"I sent myself here for an eye patch."

"You go on pretending that these are unrelated events. I'll be over here, being right."

I took her into the small bathroom. The light was almost done, flickering every few seconds. I sat her on the closed toilet and ran a few paper towels under warm water. "Okay," I said to her, "open up."

As I got close to her, I could smell the pepper oil, like faint gasoline. It didn't burn my eye or throat. Hild opened her eyes, and they were so bloodshot that all the lines looked like highways on old maps. Or she was the map. I bet if you traced all those lines in her eyes, you'd hear her whole life story—all that love and bare-knuckle learning. You could travel through her entire biography one bloodshot line at a time until she was a newborn and her parents swaddled her in a blanket, and she was so safe, so wholly important, that it was impossible she'd ever end up in a bathroom with me.

I tore my wad of wet paper towels in half, dripped each into one of her eyes, like I was feeding a premature animal with a dropper. "Is that okay?" I asked.

"Too soon to tell," she said. "I did just pepper spray myself."

"You should stop doing that."

"If I could see you, I'd be giving you an evil eye, young man."

"I get that all the time."

"You haven't seen mine. It's legendary."

"I'll have to come back another day to check it out."

"What you're doing right now," Hild said, "is above and beyond the call of duty."

"I never served."

"You're serving right now," she said.

I let more droplets fall into her raw eyes. "I'm sorry this happened to you."

"It's a rare kind of shame," she said, "pepper spraying yourself."

"Here. I'm going to dry them now." I used a couple of clean towels to carefully pat her eyes. "How does it feel?"

She squeezed her eyes. "It feels awful."

"Better and awful? Or the same and awful?" I asked.

That made Hild laugh. "Better and awful. Welcome to twenty-first-century America."

"Do you want to open your eyes and see if they're all good?" I asked.

She sat there with her shut eyes. "Not yet. This is nice and peaceful. Hopefully, no one's out there stealing stuff."

Ten seconds later, I said, "Come on. Let's try."

"Easy for you to say." She tried to open them, blinking, quickly at first, then slowing, finally stopping.

We looked right at each other, two people, three eyes, big beating hearts thumping. Then she smiled at me, huge yellow teeth that were so beautiful they almost brought me to my knees right there in the bathroom. I loved it when life gave us this kind of whiplash. One minute, we were blind, and if somebody helped us, we could see.

"So much better," said Hild. "You are a true saint."

"I've been called a lot of things before—"

"Pick whatever eye patch you want," Hild interrupted. "On the house."

"I'll stop by and visit you soon," I said. "So I can witness this legendary evil eye."

"I'd like that," she said.

I walked toward the front of the store, perused the eye patches. Most were your standard pirate fare, but one said PORN STAR across it. I snatched it and put it on. Examined myself in a little dirty mirror there for customers to ogle their decisions.

I was happy.

I was Saint.

Then Hild called from the bathroom: "And, Saint, you can take a complimentary machete!"

# 3

WE WERE ON OUR WAY to Stink Phinger, a haunt of metalheads over by the Oakland airport, off East Ninety-Fifth. I had no time for that hillbilly music, never been inside the place, though Dusty and I had dropped off drunken bikers there who didn't want to lay their motorcycles down on the highway after ten whiskeys.

My plan was simple: get my mitts on Toby, the booker. From there, we'd swim upstream fast. Get to Wes. Get Jesse free from his debt. And as bad as he was right now, stealing all the gear from Got Jokes and Trick, I was worse off than him before I went inside. I'd turned into a monster. That was what I loved about punk rock: It blocked off all the phantoms screaming in my head.

Once I got pinched, I kicked in county. There were too many junkies in there for anyone to really care. They skittered a few methadone on the floor every morning and let the withdrawing animals fight it out.

With a clear head, I finally met myself, maybe for the first time. I was clean in a cage.

That was why I wanted to help Jesse. I could help him kick. I could do for him what county did for me: sprung me from a coffin made of needles and reanimated my remains.

Most cons didn't have grateful feelings about being locked up, but I had one or two.

ᚹ

We screeched up at two in the afternoon. Stink Phinger was flanked on both sides by strip clubs, one featuring female dancers, one with men—and not the fancy kind. No lavish ads out front of tanned meat. These were rooms where you traced a lady's cesarean scar while you sobbed on her lap, where the male strippers had ankle bracelets beaming their whereabouts to parole officers. Or that was what they would have been like if the clubs hadn't gone out of business. Both buildings had been boarded up. Posted notices announced their demolitions and rebirths. I left Jesse squirming in the back seat, dope sick and begging God for the antidote.

The front door to Stink Phinger had a barstool propping it open. It had the usual fixtures of a nightclub during the day. Someone behind the bar married liquor bottles, another cut citrus, one mopped. You could hear a vacuum somewhere, singing the blues. A dejected soundman waddled about the stage, wrapping cables, caught in his daily meditation of wondering why his own band didn't break.

Someone was on the phone, shouting, sitting at the bar by herself.

This was a tall woman. About sixty, dressed to the nines in a black gown. It didn't make sense seeing someone gussied up like that here—and who was she yelling at?

She cupped her hand over the phone when she saw me come in. "We open at five," she said to me.

"I'm looking for Toby."

"Great, we open at five."

I flashed the machete at her. "It's a private matter."

She pointed at the phone, then said to me, "I'll wrap this up."

She went back to yelling at that invisible person. She sounded like my mother. And as I made that connection, I took a good look around this metalhead bar. Black walls covered in stickers. Pool tables so crooked they looked like on-ramps. And an ancient *Ms. Pac-Man* machine from the eighties.

The bar looked like the place my mom did her final routine.

ᚦ

1996.

Phoenix, Arizona.

A drunk woman danced on the bar. She had a cast on her wrist.

She was, say, in her early thirties.

She was, say, feeling no pain.

And she screamed at the bartender, "What, you don't believe me? Do you know who I am?"

It was the summer, and the TV in the bar played the Olympics—right now, showing women's gymnastics, live from Atlanta.

My mom had broken her wrist a couple days ago, had fallen in our bathroom, and coincidentally, that was also the day that a female gymnast toppled off the balance beam in the Olympics and broke hers, too. My mother never missed an opportunity to capitalize on the misfortunes of others and immediately hatched a plan to drive us to many of our usual haunts, pretending to be this injured gymnast. Even the bartenders who didn't believe her bought her a round on the house for originality.

And now, she was on this bar screaming. There was no mixer in Mom. No, she was all booze, and at the faintest slight, something so dim that nobody else could even see, she'd get mean.

So:

It didn't make any sense to her why all the other bartenders bought her free drinks, and this guy didn't think he had to—because he was special?—no one in this world was special, she used to say—so she said to the bartender, "Do you need to see me perform?" and he said, "Do I need to cut you off again?"

Meanwhile I was in the corner drinking 7UP and playing *Ms. Pac-Man*. I was very good. The game's ghosts were chasing me, and I sped through the maze. The Mexican restaurant next door gave me free baskets of chips, and here was my system: dip a chip in the 7UP, salt the chip, pop it into my mouth. My mother was chewing on something, too, yet another perceived slight, and she was giving herself some bad advice, her specialty, and suddenly, she took off her heels, and then she used her cast to climb up onto the bar, and the bartender said, "Stop it, goddamn it," but by now she was kicking over the cocktails of the other customers—they were getting wet, getting heated—she was up there having the time of her life, and I dipped a chip, salted it, and sometimes I'd unplug the *Ms. Pac-Man* machine and I'd run over to Mom and tell her that something was wrong, I needed her help, and she'd storm over and plug the machine in and tell me to stop being dumb, and now I dipped and salted a chip, popping it in my mouth, and now I was running away from a red ghost, and my mother was still on the bar and said to the bartender, "Look, I'm in the Olympics!" and she did a cartwheel, not a pretty one, almost falling off, feet slipping because of the spilled drinks, and the bartender said, "Be careful," and that red ghost gained on me, as I sped to a power pellet, almost there, and the ghost got me, and maybe I needed to unplug the machine right then, maybe I needed to call over to Mom how much I wanted her, how I needed more from her than cans of fruit cocktail and SpaghettiOs, how scary it was when I'd found her on the bathroom floor, right after falling and breaking that wrist, getting twisted up in her own undies getting undressed, breaking a bone and gashing her forehead, and she was laughing laughing laughing when I found her, and now she was laughing laughing laughing on that bar, and she said, "Where's my gold medal, Wally?" and the bartender said, "I'll call the cops," and she said, "Just buy me a drink, you cheap bastard, and I'll come down," and he said, "No," and she said, "The show must go on!" and I looked at the TV and it was now showing shots of Olympic Village, all these happy athletes and their smiling families, and they were all there, doing their best, and I was here watching her routine on the bar, a never-ending river of rank fruit cocktail and a moat of SpaghettiOs, and I couldn't stand another second, no, I didn't need to unplug this *Ms. Pac-Man* machine and beg my mother for attention, no, I couldn't make her love me more than liquor, no, we were going to dance on bars forever unless I decided to make my life better, yes, I needed to flee, I was gonna get to the Olympic Village now.

So I ran out of the bar.

Down the block.

I didn't turn around to see if she came after me.

I didn't want to know.

That was one thing Ms. Pac-Man didn't have to worry about. They were always coming for her.

I ran to the nearest intersection and put my thumb out to hitchhike to Atlanta, to Olympic Village, to all those happy families who never drank that sweet piss from their fruit cocktail cans for dessert.

Þ

"Okay, sorry," the gowned woman at Stink Phinger said to me, hanging up the phone. "I make it a policy to never keep someone with a blade waiting."

"Where's Toby?"

"I'm Amy."

"Where's Toby, Amy?"

"Back there," she said, hopping off her stool, strutting in that black gown, leading me through a door marked GUARD DOG. We walked down a narrow hall, by all the warm kegs of beer, into an office—but nobody was there. And I never saw a pooch.

The lady crashed behind the desk.

I stayed standing.

"You're pretty calm about this machete thing," I said.

"I make love to pressure," she said. "A poet said that. Or a basket-ball player."

"Are you gonna get Toby?"

"I can't."

"Why not?"

"There is no Toby."

"I'm not the one to do this with."

"I mean, there is a Toby—but it's me. I'm Toby."

"You're Amy."

"I own this place as Amy. I book as Toby. Rock and roll is so sexist that it's easier when bands think a dude books the shows." Amy looked at the machete again. "What were you gonna do if I was a guy?"

"I was going to threaten to cut your hand off."

"What if he called your bluff?"

"What if I cut off his hand?"

"What's your name?" she said.

"I tell you I'm going to cut off somebody's hand, and you want to know my name?"

"Yeah," said Amy, "I want to know who you are."

I was starting to like this lady. She was sick with recklessness, like me.

Þ

I figured every car would want to stop for an eight-year-old as I tried to flag one down, but it took a few minutes before someone stopped. A woman in a station wagon. "Are you okay?" she said, rolling her window down only halfway, stopping at the level of her nose.

"I'm hitchhiking."

"That's strange for your age," she said, her breath making the window fog up.

"I need to get to Atlanta."

"Oh, I'm not going that far," she said, laughing, using her hand to clear the glass.

"My mom is there. She's a gymnast. In the Olympics."

She lowered her window down all the way. "Wow! That's impressive," she said. "What's her name?"

"She doesn't use her real name."

"And your dad? Where's he?" she asked.

"He's in Norway."

"Who are you with now, honey?"

"I'm going to Olympic Village," I said. "They're expecting me."

"Can I take you somewhere around here?"

"When I get there, we're having a party."

"That sounds nice," she said, "but I can't leave you on the street—and I can't drive you to Georgia."

"Atlanta."

"Right," she said, sighing, "so what should we do?"

I thought about it a minute. "Atlanta is east."

"That's true."

"Please take me as far east as you can, without going out of your way. I'll keep getting rides until I get there."

"You're polite," she said. "Okay, I'll get you as close as I can," and I got in, and we drove off, and I remember thinking that the station wagon was like Ms. Pac-Man and the roads were the mazes and we needed to outrun those ghosts.

"How old is your mom?" she said.

"Thirty-four."

"That's old for a gymnast, isn't it?"

"She's the best there is."

"What's her name?"

"I told you. She uses a fake name."

"What's her fake name?"

I didn't know what to say. Nothing came to me. I knew lots of women's names, but I couldn't remember one of them sitting in her station wagon, the one with the fogged window because somebody stopped to help me.

"I'm worried about you," she said.

"I'm tired," I said. "And hungry."

That lady didn't drive me east at all, didn't get me close to Olympic Village. She took me to the police station. When we got there, all the officers were huddled around a TV. There had been a bombing at the Olympics. People were dead. People were hurt.

"Did it hit the Olympic Village?" I asked a cop.

"I don't know," he said, "but it's bad."

I figured the cops would take me straight home—that I'd hear it from Mom about running off. Or she wouldn't even remember what went down.

That happened, too.

We often played a game over oatmeal in the morning: Did That Happen? I'd give her true or false quizzes about our adventures the day before. I'd tell her all sorts of crazy things, and some were real, some were fictions, and some broke our hearts, but on most of those mornings, we always found a way to laugh about it all.

That was how breakfast would start tomorrow: *Hey, Mom, true or false: Did you do gymnastics on the bar to prove you were an injured Olympian?*

And if I ate a *Ms. Pac-Man* power pellet of courage: *Hey, Mom, true or false: Were you ever going to take care of me?*

But it didn't matter.

None of those things.

It turned out that the cops couldn't take me home.

And it turned out that we'd never play Did That Happen? again; she'd never answer any of my questions. Because the bomb in Atlanta wasn't the only one that went off.

See, after I split the bar, my mom tried to do a big gymnastics grand finale. She slipped and fell, smacked her skull so hard it turned into a soft-boiled egg, her liquor-thinned yolk pouring onto the bar's linoleum.

I didn't have a mother anymore.

And all that shit I thought I wanted to leave behind when I'd run out of the dive bar earlier, I wanted it all back. I only ever wanted to eat tortilla chips and drink flat 7UP. I only ever wanted to skip school and go on day-drunks with her, only ever wanted to dance to Madonna on the jukebox and laugh so hard. I only ever wanted to watch her come in my room at night and weep on the floor. And there was nothing wrong with SpaghettiOs, and there was nothing wrong with that embalming fluid called fruit cocktail. I wanted to play *Ms. Pac-Man* until the world ended, and I wanted to hear her yell at Wally, and I wanted to watch her do gymnastics, please, let me have all that, please, give it back to me.

I'm sorry I left, Mom, will you please come back?

I'm sorry I left, Mom, will you please?

I'm sorry I left, Mom.

I'm sorry.

ᚦ

Amy was evaluating the look in my one blue eye. "Come on," she said, "what's your name?" Then she stared at my PORN STAR eye patch. "Who are you?"

I hadn't planned on saying it, but it just rang out: "Saint."

And can I tell you how it felt hearing it leak from my lips for the first time? It was like writing a song. I always started with the riff, dialing in its growl, that balance of teeth and tenderness. Then I'd find the melody to sing over it. Once it was right, that was all I wanted to do that whole day, play it, sing it, over and over. Nothing made me happier than finishing a new song.

The day before, it didn't exist. Shit, even a few hours earlier, it was just a word I'd never associated with myself, *saint*, until Hild said it.

And now, the song was alive.

Now, I was Saint.

That was how it felt to say it: the thrill of discovering life.

"I didn't know saints carried machetes," she said, and I was going to have to get used to that, jokes about my new name.

"So you own this place?" I asked.

"Three years now."

"And you work with Wes Than Zero?"

Her posture changed, shoulders slumping. "Right, I knew it would happen eventually," she said with a sigh, picking up some cigarettes and lighting one, even offering one to me, which was nice. I shook my head no. "I knew sooner or later this day would come. Let's just handle this as straight business. Let me write you a check. How much did he take you for?"

"How can you steal from struggling bands?"

"I never took anything."

"Wes must have kicked you back a percentage, right?"

"That's business between him and me."

"I'd answer my questions."

"Be careful with him," she said. "He'll jack you up."

I understood why Wes would be scary to other people. But I had spent time in Norway, where my father turned me into a real deal Viking. Where the boy from the New World met the old one. Whatever Amy thought her day was going to be, it was something else now, something that would get me to Wes. "I need something from you," I said.

"I'm not going to like this at all, am I?"

"I'd be surprised."

"Gimme a sec." She fumbled for her cigarettes on the desk, retrieved another, lit it, and held one in each of her hands, alternating drags. It was like somebody on their first day in rehab, so stressed in this new reality that the only thing they wanted was to disappear in a cloud of smoke.

"Are you ready?" I asked.

"Rip the Band-Aid."

"You're going to set up a meeting for me with Wes."

She hit both smokes at once, blew out a fogbank. "I understand that you think you want that, but you don't. Trust me."

"I can't trust somebody who steals from musicians."

"And what if I refuse?" she asked.

"Don't refuse. That's the machete talking, not me."

She took another double drag. "Your machete is an asshole." She put out both smokes, sitting in her swivel chair, glowering at me.

I really liked her, not giving an inch to the machete and me. I admired that bravery, but it was being wasted in petty crime. There were plenty of worms in the world to slum with instead of Wes Than Zero. The look in this lady's eyes meant she could be more.

"I need to know something about you," I said to her. "Did you only get in bed with Wes because he threatened you?"

"Why does it matter now?"

"I need to know the truth," I said.

"He was in my home."

"So you were scared."

"Of course I was fucking scared."

I wanted to believe what Amy said. I wanted to believe that she got into this business for the right reasons, to make a good living, sure, but also because she loved music. If that sounded naive of me, it was willful, and it was an okay life, being willfully naive to the things that broke your heart.

"I'm going to ask another question," I said, "and I hope you're honest. I don't mean that in a threatening way. I hope you'll tell me the truth."

She lit another cigarette, just one this time, and swiveled in her chair from side to side, eyeballing me in her ball gown. "What is it?"

Maybe, in a way, I was the bomb going off at her Olympics. Maybe, in a way, I was the bar she fell off that turned her brain to chili. I was certainly here to change her life.

"Did Wes pay you, too?"

She could barely hold the cigarette in her hand. I could see it in her eyes: She yearned to be able to lie, but something in the moment wouldn't let her do it. "Yes."

"And you knew he was stealing from the bands?"

"Yes."

"And do you want to keep being a piece of shit?"

"No."

"Are you lying to me?"

"No," she said.

And one more time: I wanted to believe what Amy said. Wanted to be in this office with somebody who ached to smash this body cast she'd been forced inside of—and it was a hard one to escape because it was made of money.

She was telling the truth about being afraid of Wes.

She was also telling the truth about taking his payoffs.

And she was telling the truth with a look in her eyes that meant she could be better than this.

I'd met a Buddhist in Quentin who told me about the terrible twins, happiness and unhappiness. Each one had half the universe. Equal shares of all those light-years. Equal shares of us.

So I said to the terrible twins of Amy, "I'm going to help you."

# 4

AMY'S HOUSEBOAT was over in Sausalito.
She'd have to move soon. In fact, she was the only boat left in this little marina. The ownership had changed hands, and the fascists were tearing it down. Supposedly, they were promising to rebuild it, but Amy had serious doubts.

"I bet it's waterfront condos next year," she said.

Since she was the only boat moored at the docks, the parking lot was totally empty. We walked on creaking planks to her place. The sun was teasing us behind gauzy curtains of fog.

Her boat was small. You entered right into her living room, which fed into a galley. From there, a tiny bathroom and a bedroom.

Successful bands had bigger tour buses, but the wall art was amazing: all old concert posters from the '70s. That acid-style, stoner chic. Talking Heads. Kiss. Neil Young. ZZ Top. The Velvet Underground.

I liked this cramped boat a lot, though I despised Sausalito and all of Marin County. All you needed to know about it was that the residents here kept voting down bringing BART into their precious North Bay because people like me might go over. People thought it was a race thing, and sure, that was a component. But it was really class. Black, brown, white—they didn't want us poor people rooting through their golden garbage cans.

If my old man could see me on this boat, he'd say, *Our bones are boats*, and he'd mean Norway. Norse pagans. We had warriors in our bloodstream.

He gave me a sword on the day I moved in with him. Before he'd even said, *Hello, I'm your father whom you've never met, and I'm so sorry that your mother is dead*, he handed me the weapon and said, "You master this sword, and you can bring it with you to Valhalla."

A machete wasn't a sword.

A houseboat wasn't a longship.

But I did feel the Vikings in me. They were all getting ready.

"You need to let Wes know that the club is under new management," I said to Amy, "and tell him I'm not interested in keeping your arrangement going."

"I don't know how to get in touch with him."

"You expect me to believe that you don't have his number?"

"I don't."

"Jesse told me Wes emailed you when he first made contact."

"Yeah, and he said never to use it," she said. "He said that there'd be . . . consequences, if I did."

"We can email him now," I said.

"He's been in my house."

"I know that."

"He'll kill me at worst, and if I'm lucky, I wake up in the hospital."

We both knew that she was right. Once contact had been made, she needed to be sequestered away. Maybe I could put some distance between them. I wasn't going to be able to play nurse to withdrawing Jesse all day. If Amy helped with him, then I could claim Stink Phinger as the field of battle, setting up a showdown with Wes. If he didn't know how to find Amy, she'd be safe.

"Then let's email him now," I said.

"He'll kill me."

"I'm not going to let that happen."

"Says the guy Wes doesn't want to kill."

"I'm hoping he wants me dead within the hour."

"Maybe we can go halfsies on a joint burial plot," said Amy, lighting two more cigarettes for herself.

"Where's your computer?" I asked.

"I don't really have a choice, do I?" She let both smokes dangle from her lips, skinny little cancer tusks.

I told her what the plan was—that I'd let Wes know that I was in charge now, and that in order to hide Amy, she would have to help me with Jesse.

"I don't want to take care of a junkie even a little bit," she said.

I tried giving her a sympathetic look, but it was a tough sell with only one good eye and a PORN STAR eye patch over the other.

"And I'm also going to need the deed to your club," I said.

She ripped both tusks from her maw. "My deed?! Why?"

"To keep you on my side," I said, "and to keep Wes focused on me, not you."

I was pillaging by taking her deed. But it was "good" pillaging. I needed leverage over Amy. This was the way for me to make things right. Plundering had such a tricky reputation. Everything had its time and place. Even Green Day sounded all right in Whole Foods.

From her wall safe in her bedroom, Amy pulled out the deed. There were clothes all over the floor and the bed was unmade. The place stunk of mildew. This was the part where she should've handed the document to me. Instead, she asked, "Is there another way?"

"I could threaten you, if that's easier. Make it seem like you don't have a choice."

"I don't have a choice."

"For example," I said, "I could say that if you don't give me the deed, I'll sink your houseboat."

"Jesus, you're mean."

"Me?!"

"Uh, yeah, you're a boat sinker and a machete wielder. Do those sound like good qualities to you?"

"In your case, I'm being exceedingly nice."

"I guarantee you that in heaven, there isn't a secret club filled with all the good people who sink boats and carry machetes."

"There is in Valhalla."

"So you're stealing my club."

"I'm trying to keep you safe," I said.

She looked at me with desperation. "I don't want to give you my deed."

"We're here, Amy, because of a choice that you made. This is how we start to fix things."

"I'm not proud of what I did. It didn't bother me at all when you called me a piece of shit because I say that to myself every morning."

But she still wasn't coughing the deed up.

I needed to clarify something to Amy: "It isn't I'll sink the boat *or* take the deed. I'm saying if you don't hand me the deed right now, the boat will sink as well."

"Oh," she said, "I thought it was one or the other."

"I should've been clearer."

"I'd say."

Maybe my PORN STAR eye patch had some luck in it, too—not as much as my old fake eye, but at least a shake of stardust. Because the way this was working out, I didn't have to hurt anyone, and I didn't have to live with more violence.

"This is brutal," she said, then handed over the deed. "Let's just get all this over with so I can go feel sorry for myself."

She went and snatched her laptop, opened her email, handed it to me. "Do you mind if I shower while you're ruining my life?" she asked. "I was at the club all night. This dress smells like a body bag."

"It's only BO."

"Yeah, well, you have personality BO. Stealing my club—"

"I'm helping you."

"So let me take a goddamn shower."

I wasn't an unreasonable man. And I understood why she thought she'd just lost her club. There was no way for her to know that I didn't want it, that she'd get it back once this was over. I could squawk that truth till I was having an asthma attack and she'd never believe me.

I checked out the bathroom to make sure there wasn't a way for her to slip out a window, make a run for it. I riffled drawers and peeked around for stashed weapons. All good. "Go on, clean yourself up."

"Thanks."

"But I'm going to sit outside the bathroom door the whole time."

"No peeking."

"I'm not like that."

Amy looked right into my good eye: "You know what? I actually believe that about you. I won't try and escape," she said. "I'm too tired."

Then she shut herself in the bathroom and turned on the water.

I sat in the hall, leaning on the closed door, blocking it, just in case.

I emailed Wes Than Zero, short and sweet:

*I'm running Amy's shop now. Stink Phinger is mine. Call me to negotiate new terms.*

Amy sang in the shower, belting out "Me & Mr. Jones" by Amy Winehouse. It felt too familiar, her trusting me with a song, letting me sit in this concert, but I was thrilled to be the only one in the audience at her speakeasy.

"You're a good singer!" I shouted through the door.

"What?"

"You're a good singer!"

"What?"

Now I really yelled: "Never! Mind! Just! Keep! Singing!"

Amy, the bad pillager, broke back into the same song, while I, the good pillager, sat on her boat. We could marvel at anything we wanted to in these little lives, and at that moment, Amy worked for Bragi, the Norse god of music. Amy was welcoming all the fallen warriors into paradise.

ᚦ

We were an odd carpool, no doubt. I drove the Reliant from 1906, Amy rode next to me, Jesse moaned from the back seat, lying on his side in the fetal position and sweating. We were on the Richmond–San Rafael Bridge, heading east. If the freeways cooperated, we would be back to Sound Check in a half hour.

Temporarily, the sky turned blue, though you could see great tufts over the ocean. The fog would come for us soon, but for now, the sun was out, and I got the Reliant up to seventy, which seemed to test its limits, the chassis quaking.

Soon, we fed onto 80, a highway that rarely cooperated. Always snarled. Always merging. Gangs of semis blowing tires, leaving those carcasses on the side of the road looking like dead seals.

We slowed to twenty, passing the racetrack.

Amy turned around to face Jesse, staring at his anguish and talking to me: "He's withdrawing or giving birth?"

"He's going to have a rough couple days."

"Join the club," Amy said to him.

Jesse raised his head from its perch. There was spit hanging from his chin. "Wait. Who's she?"

I paused, wondering if I should tell him the truth. "That's Toby," I said to him, "and Amy."

"You can call me Amy," she said to him.

"It feels like there's a jellyfish inside stinging my guts," he said, then passed out again.

"I guess I'm having a better day than him," said Amy. "Barely."

"I'm sorry if I've been a prick," I said to Amy.

"Oh, you've been a prick—but it's not your fault. It's like I drank a glass of poison and now I'm blaming it for killing me."

I made a face like somebody trying to do math in his head.

"Wait. I'm the poison?" I asked, and she said, "You said it, not me."

Þ

As we reached West Oakland and pulled into Sound Check's parking lot, Dusty met me outside and said, "We have a problem, and that problem has a sledgehammer."

"Who has a sledgehammer?" I asked, getting out of the Reliant. The wastewater funk flung some rotten eggs up my nose.

"Trick Wilma."

The thing about Sound Check was that bands came and went, seven days, twenty-four-hour access. So some people you knew, and some you never saw. I'd never met Trick, only admired her singing and bass playing in All the Fuss, shaking through our shared wall.

"Why is she our problem?" I asked.

"Do you remember," Dusty said, scratching at his dustache, a habit I'd long thought he exaggerated to draw attention to his outstanding facial hair, "how their band used to be our neighbor?"

"Used to be?"

"We're more like . . . roommates now." Then Dusty saw Jesse and Amy in the Reliant. "Who's that lady?"

"That's another problem we have," I said.

"And yet another problem is Jesse being here at all. Trick is breathing fire about their gear getting ganked. She'll kill him. Seriously."

"I've never actually met Trick," I said.

"Well, good news—she's batshit."

"I like people who are batshit," I said. "I'm batshit."

"Then it's your lucky day," said Dusty.

I followed him into Sound Check's hall. The walls were all covered with carpet scraps and egg cartons, the occasional ironic poster of a glam band. Winger was especially well represented. We entered our wrecked room, and there had been a storm of sorts, a blizzard of drywall swirling in the air. It was dusted all over the ground, too. There was a "door" connecting our two practice rooms the size of a couple of vending machines.

Trick was screaming: "Is that him, Dusty? Is that fucking him?" and she stormed over, planting the sledgehammer on her shoulder, looking every bit a punk rock Valkyrie.

She was tattooed, full sleeves, a job stopper of a blood-tipped dagger on her neck, and had a tangle of matted pink hair. Trick Wilma was the kind of woman you married in the dayroom of a mental hospital. You honeymooned in a dumpster, lived in a converted mousetrap, and despite the obvious squalor, the union was the best decision you ever made.

She didn't have a drop of Green Day in her.

Her band would be great without Got Jokes. You couldn't play punk rock with him. He'd pose as gutter long enough to have stories to tell his inevitable, suburban softball team. Please. He was so boring he should give people forced to talk to him an EpiPen to stay awake. The only thing checkered about his past were those stupid Vans he wore.

"How could you do this?" she said to me. Then she noticed my new PORN STAR eye patch. "Whoa. You didn't have that patch last time I saw you in the hall."

"I don't remember meeting you."

"We didn't. I said I saw you in the hall. What happened to your eye?"

I respected that, being in that zone of spontaneous violence and still making sure I was all right.

"Gave my fake eye away," I said.

"Why did you give your eye away?"

"Someone needed it more than me."

"That's the craziest shit anyone's ever said—and I'm having a bad day, too, thanks for fucking asking," she said, taking the sledge and hitting another hole in the wall, remembering that she hated me. "This morning, my band had gear for our gig tonight. We also had a guitarist with two working hands."

"Right," I said, "about that."

She threw the sledge down and lunged at me, slapping me across the face.

It was fine.

My temper didn't even stir.

"I wouldn't do that," Dusty said to her.

"Do you know how hard I worked for this show?" she yelled at me, trying to hit me again, but I slipped the shot. "I put everything into this set, into these songs!"

I put my hands up between us, slow, passive. "I know. And I'm sorry. I lost my temper at him."

"Do you know how often I want to break his hand?" she asked me. "I want to break his hand multiple times a day—often several times an hour—but I don't do it."

Got Jokes yelped from the other room: "Dude, I can hear you, babe!"

As if in answer, she retrieved and wielded the sledgehammer expertly, putting another hole in the wall and launching another drywall plume.

"I'm gonna get your gear back for you," I said to Trick.

"That's *one* thing you're going to do for me."

I turned to Dusty. "What does she mean by that?"

"Our list of problems swells," said Dusty.

"You're playing guitar for us tonight, too," she said to me. "Got Jokes can still sing his backups. I play bass and sing. Our drummer is outside, ready to go, assuming we have drums she can play."

"She can use our drummer's gear," I said.

"You're not taking the Jawbreaker show away from me," Trick said to me, then went back to banging the sledgehammer into the wall, calling to me, "You fucked my life! That's what you did today! You, life fucker! But I'm not going to let you fuck it!"

I peered at her through a cloud of toxic white dust. I loved her madness. This woman with a sledgehammer, she'd slapped me in the face, and it was perfect.

She kept the sledge swinging now, breaking the walls, screaming, "You can un-fuck this! And you're going to un-fuck this!" She had almost knocked down the entire wall between our practice spaces. "Or I can fuck you, too. I can make Got Jokes press charges. See, you can't say no! See, I've got you by the nuts!"

And I thought, *Now I know what Amy felt.*

I was quickly losing sight of Trick with all the poisonous snow in the air.

I was quickly losing sight of everything.

"I'll knock this whole room down!" she said. "I'll hit the whole building! I'll knock down your house!"

Finally, Trick stopped swinging. I wanted to kiss her before she put that hammer down, wanted to feel her strong tongue in my mouth. I reached out to where I thought she was and only grasped dust. Then I glimpsed her again, barely.

She was a shape.

She was a sledgehammer.

"You have about eight hours to learn nine songs," she said to me, which only made me want to kiss her more. "You'll learn the songs and you'll kick ass at the gig tonight, do you understand that, asshole? You aren't going to fucking ruin this for me."

Maybe there was a way to say no to a Valkyrie.

Maybe that language existed somewhere.

But nobody had taught it to me.

# 5

YOU'RE A PERSON who has this song, the very first song of Trick Wilma's, storming into your ears, pure punk rock energy, un-varnished psychosis, un-airbrushed and untamed, drywall particles defying physics, riding secret gusts of notes belching from amps, moving weightless like tiny drunken astronauts, and Trick led us with her bass lines, and the drummer who didn't have a name hit those skins so hard they must've owed her money, and Got Jokes sat in the other now connected room singing his backups, unseen, avoiding me and my temper and a certain proclivity to break hands, and the point was that Trick and I were together, I played guitar and she growled, alive in this drywall tundra, this snow globe, this sleet and sleaze, this squall, this fuss, this tempest, this bomb cyclone, this ice storm, this out-of-tune Valhalla.

ᚦ

I flew to Norway three days after my mother's death and was picked up at the Alesund Airport by Gudrun, who worked for my father. "I do everything for him except blow the glass," she said. After that, she didn't talk to me the rest of the ride but bargained with her sister on the phone over which of them would check on their demented mother.

It was an hour ride to his cabin and studio, situated on a plain, with a fjord cutting it in half. We were surrounded by green hills, and I couldn't see another house in any direction. His place was a ramshackle one-story structure, its wooden walls faded to gray and beige. The barn/studio, by contrast, was painted bright red, with state-of-the-art equipment inside for his glassblowing. Scattered in the yard, there were all kinds of broken machinery. A punching bag. A bale of hay with a target on it for archery.

It might be called a salvage yard, but it didn't look like there was much to save. There was a garden, though. Rows of corn. Potatoes and carrots. I'd learn later that the potatoes weren't for eating—he made wine from them, the same way as the Vikings. The only items that seemed to be of any value were these glass birds, opulent, colorful. Some were suspended from wire hangers. Others lay on top of other junk. But they were the most beautiful things I'd ever seen.

It would be weeks until I learned that he made them. That he blew the glass in his studio and bent them into these elaborate, vibrant, graceful shapes, wings out in flight, feather textures rippling and dappling the thin glass—and he painted flourishes of bright colors. Turns out people paid thousands and waited years to get one of his glass birds. They hung in museums around the world. Priceless, his birds, and here was a flock of them, crashed among all the junk. Even when I was finally made aware of his reputation, I could never spot a hint of hubris or ego in him. He was never a famous artist to me.

My first day at his house, I found him around the back, burning papers in an empty oil drum. He wore blue jeans, no shoes, no socks, no shirt. He was svelte, with sun-damaged hair, long and blond. Mom always said he looked like her favorite singer, Iggy Pop, and she was right, except my father had eight inches and seventy-five pounds on the little front man.

"Welcome to the Old World," my dad said.

That was when he rummaged around in a rickety armoire in the yard that had its doors busted off. He handed me the sword that I told you about earlier, said the thing about taking it all the way to Valhalla. Honestly, up until this trip, I didn't even know I was Norwegian. I was one of those American mutts who had no idea where they originally came from.

Also, I was only eight.

"I'll only ask you one question today," he said. "Do you think you can tell me the truth?"

"I'll try."

"That's all I want from you, boy. The truth. Sounds simple, but most people spend their lives robbing the earth of it."

"Okay."

"I'll ask you one question every day," he said, "and that way, we can get to know each other slowly."

"What am I supposed to call you?"

"My name."

"What's your name?"

He started laughing, threw another handful of papers in the fire. We watched this little spark shower zoom up from the drum, like burning grasshoppers levitating. "Are you trying to tell me that they didn't give you my name? Not even your mother?"

"Maybe—but I can't remember."

"I'm Trondur," he said, "so I've answered your question, but you haven't answered mine."

"Oh. Sorry."

"You should know my name." Then, for the first time in my life, my father smiled at me. "Are you ready to hear my question?"

"Okay . . . Trondur."

"Good pronunciation. We'll have you speaking our language in no time."

"Okay."

"You're finally home. Here—help me burn all this." He gave me a handful of crumpled-up pages. I wanted to open one, see what was on it. But I didn't want to anger this large, shirtless man, Trondur, my father—

Yes, I had a father, and we were together.

"Call me Tron," he said.

"Okay."

"Our first question, and remember, I always want you to tell me the truth: Are you a pagan prince, born to defend your people?"

"What's pagan?"

"We'll start your education there."

ᛈ

I told Trick and Got Jokes that I needed to talk to Dusty out front for a couple minutes, get our signals straight for the rest of the day. He and I exited Sound Check. The sky, that big ol' tease, had taken back its blue and replaced it with fog. Meanwhile, Amy had helped Jesse out of the car, and now he was puking in the bushes. She held back his stringy hair, like a responsible sorority sister.

Just as I was about to begin the conversation with Dusty, some cars screamed from 880, tires shrieking like anxious monkeys. (Because of the industrial shops set up around Sound Check and how secluded this part of West Oakland was after dark, cops were always finding stolen cars parked around here, husks, stripped bones. I saw one once that had a tag scribbled across its windshield, written in lipstick: LOVE LIVED HERE. I didn't know why that tag had burrowed into me so extravagantly, but I couldn't stop thinking about it; for weeks, it tumbled across my brain like impossible philosophy. Was it meant as reveal? Was it LOVE LIVED HERE, and whoever scribbled was talking about how lucky they had been, blessed—yes, life could be lonely, and bills could be past due, and the repo man was coming for your car, but through it all, maybe because of all that life noise, love lived here? Or was it grim? LOVE LIVED HERE, right up until it was totaled, bent and unrecognizable, repair unbearable. One minute, it was here and important, and then it was mauled. Or maybe the person who wrote it just wasn't good with tenses, and they were bragging, wanted everybody who walked by to know that this vehicle carried only one thing, a singular affection, just theirs, whoever they were, wherever they went. The tag had that Rorschach uncertainty. You read that lipsticked line and learned something about yourself by what you thought it meant. LOVE LIVED HERE. What would you have made of its secret code?)

As the squealing tires receded, I pointed to Amy, still holding the retching Jesse's hair, and said to Dusty, "She's been working with the man behind the whole hustle."

"So what do you want to do?" Dusty asked.

"Stay on the move with them. I can't take the chance that he gets his hands on her or Jesse. He's dangerous. And I'll call you as soon as I talk to him."

"Do you know his name?" Dusty said.

"Goes by Wes Than Zero."

Dusty made a face I'd never seen before—and since we spent so much time together, I thought I knew all his faces. But I didn't trust this new mask of self-preservation. It was a face covered with tree bark.

"Then we've got a new problem," said Dusty. "Wes is my supplier."

Amy helped Jesse into the car, walking arm in arm. She climbed in, too. They seemed like they were having a heart-to-heart in the back seat. She leaned over and hugged him.

"That's good news you know him," I said to Dusty. "You can get me to him quick."

Dusty didn't say anything for ten seconds, then repeated, "Wes is my supplier."

Amy was now consoling Jesse. He was being ravaged from the inside out. I knew his stomach felt like lava, gurgling and angry, and yet his skin was frosty. I remembered the terror of early withdrawal. It made everything a gigantic hallucination, a horror movie that hated you.

I kept watching Amy comforting somebody she just met. How bad could she really be? Sure, she got caught up in Wes's cruelty, but here she was helping a stranger, while Dusty, my friend, did the opposite.

"Are you telling me that you're with Wes on this?" I asked him.

"I'm telling you that he's my supplier."

"Yes, that particular message has been successfully delivered."

"Go easy, Ja—"

He started to say my old name, so I had to stop him: "Saint. My new name is Saint."

"Wait, what?" Dusty said. "You changed your name today?"

"It was . . . a gift."

"From who?"

In one of those Quentin writing classes, I'd been taught when to use *who* versus *whom*, but it wasn't the time for grammar.

"A new friend," I said.

"You changed your name because of a new friend?! Like legally? You really have a new name?"

He'd left me no choice: "*Whom.*"

"What?"

"You said 'from who,' but it's *whom.*"

"So whom gave you this new name?" Dusty asked.

That was still not grammatically correct, though I'd keep this last one to myself.

We were usually so synced up. Not just grinding in his cab—when we played music, too. We had that chemistry, that anticipation. All we needed was eye contact, and we could follow changes in songs that we wrote on the fly. It was a kind of sonic telepathy.

"I'm not with Wes, *Saint*," Dusty said, frowning. "Let me talk to him first. That's all I'm asking."

"Jesse and Amy told me everything. What else is there to know?"

"I want to hear it from him," Dusty said. "That's all I'm doing here. Let's talk after I—"

"I'm putting him out of business." I pointed over at crying Jesse in the car. "And Wes wants to kill him tomorrow."

"The salary I pay you for working in the cab," Dusty said, "comes from Wes's money."

"Then I quit."

"None of us got clean hands," said Dusty.

I looked at Amy one last time. Jesse's head was on her shoulder. "That's the tremendous thing about hands," I said to Dusty. "You can scrub them. You can live clean."

"I'll go talk to him now."

"Take me along."

"I can't do that."

"You can do whatever you want," I said. "You can even tell him that the club is mine."

"What does that mean?"

I pulled the deed out of my pocket and showed it to him. "I'm a small business owner. I guess this is the American dream."

Right then, Trick walked into the parking lot and said, "Hey, Saint, let's get back to practicing!" A split second later she spotted Jesse in Got Jokes's Reliant. Her eyes went wide, and she bounded toward the car, shrieking at Jesse, "You dream thief! You stole our dreams! Off with your head!"

About ten feet from the Reliant, Trick leaned down and picked up chunks of broken pavement and heaved them at Jesse, still safely inside Got Jokes's ride. She cracked the windshield. She bumped and scuffed the paint. A dent here. Another there. She made it hail pavement.

Got Jokes came outside, too, saw the carnage, and said, "Babe! My car! Dude, babe, not cool!"

I couldn't help it. I burst out laughing.

So did Dusty.

Trick threw a couple more rocks and then ran at the car, trying to muscle open the locked door, Trick pointing at Jesse and pounding on the window and still saying, "Off with your head, dream thief, off with your head!"

Dusty and I stood there, still laughing our asses off, forgetting our circumstances, a few seconds of wonderful anesthesia before we sobered up and remembered, yes, for a few seconds, we were two oblivious friends who would always watch the other's six.

*Love lived here.*

# 6

O N THE SECOND NIGHT living with my father, Tron shook me
on the chest, hard, in the middle of the night. "We have to go,"
he said.

I sat up from the cot I'd been bunking on. I was sweaty. I was used to
sleeping under a sheet and a shawl in Arizona's scald, but Tron had given
me a huge blanket made from a black bear. I liked being in his place. I
felt safe, as though there wasn't anything that could hurt me around my
humungous father. Did he bring this bear down himself and turn the
beast into a blanket for me?

"What's going on?" I asked.

"You need to get to know your home, your country," he said.

It was dark in the house, and Tron flipped on a flashlight, threw it to
me. "You have to keep up with me," he said, taking off toward the door
and running full speed into the darkness.

I dripped sweat from the weight of the bear blanket, my head all wonky,
but I jumped up to follow him. I sprinted through the yard—hadn't

ever been in nature like this before, hadn't lived in a place that wasn't dominated by man-made light. Out here, there was nothing to dim the sky.

I clicked off my flashlight and stared straight up. I'd seen stars that only looked white, but here, there were various colors, golden, green, blue, red. I'd seen stars that seemed cut from only one pattern, one size, but out here, some were peppercorns while others were small skulls.

I knew I was supposed to try to catch up to Tron, but I didn't know how to hurry, not under this gleaming zoo of light.

"What are you doing?" he called from the darkness. "Hurry!"

He raced and zigzagged through trees, and I tore after him, pointing my flashlight to the ground, not wanting to catch a toe on a root, a rock, fall down, crack my head—nobody had ever woken me like that, and I didn't know what we were running toward or what we were running away from. I didn't know anything except that he was going fast, and I had to keep up. His sights set on a hill, he sprinted up the grassy slope and so did I, lungs burning. We were almost to the top when Tron stopped and grabbed me so I couldn't see over to the other side.

He put his hand over my mouth. "We have to be quiet," he whispered.

"Why?"

"We don't want them to know we're here."

"Who?"

"Go on. Look over."

I crawled the last few feet and peeked over, into a valley, but what I saw made no sense. I first thought of a hundred lightsabers floating by themselves. Glowing bright yellow. Fluorescent. But they couldn't be lightsabers, because they weren't straight. They were shaped like tree branches, but ones that moved like electricity in a circuit.

I had no idea what I was looking at. I only knew that I was surrounded by light, in the sky, in the valley; by the light I felt being around Tron.

He snuck up close to me, peered over, too. "Here is today's question," said my father. "What could that possibly be down there?"

"I don't know," I said.

"Would you like to take a guess?" he asked.

"Are they aliens?"

He laughed, but not in a mean way, not like my mom. "No, not aliens," he said, pulling out a handgun that looked made of plastic. "But that's a good guess."

I pointed at the gun: "What is that for?"

"One of the problems we have in Norway," he said, "is that reindeers wander into the roads. Thousands of accidents a year. Many deaths. So some ranchers paint their reindeers' antlers with reflective paint, making it easier for drivers to see them at night. Bright paint, like what they use on highway lines. So that's what you see down there, boy. Painted antlers."

I pointed at the gun again. "Are you going to shoot them?"

He pointed the gun to the sky. "I'm going to shoot a flare, and it will spook them a little. We'll watch them dance in the light."

"Their antlers look radioactive," I said.

"They do."

"That's funny, right? Radioactive antlers."

"Okay," he said, "let's watch the show."

Tron pulled the trigger on the flare gun, and after a few seconds, a boom, then an eruption of red in the sky, all those stars temporarily overpowered. The flare was bright enough so that we could see the animals themselves down in the valley for a moment—and then the reindeer and their radioactive antlers turned into anarchy, those scared animals, the fluorescent antlers clashing like swords. It looked to me as if they threw off sparks, these beasts with bolts of lightning growing from their heads.

ᚦ

After finishing our LOVE LIVED HERE talk, Dusty drove off, fast, from Sound Check, on his way to Wes.

We were all still in the parking lot.

Got Jokes was flipping out about his newly rock-thrashed car.

Jesse and Amy remained locked inside of it, unwilling to open up. It didn't matter. I had the keys.

I said to Trick, "Maybe we can take a walk. Cool down."

She pointed through the ruined windshield at Jesse: "But I want to kill that guy."

"Which is why we should split."

She and I turned to leave, and Got Jokes called to us: "Should I come, too? Is this, like, a band thing?"

"You get Jesse out of your ride," Trick said, "because I'm still going to kick his ass."

She and I took off down Grand Avenue, the wastewater plant perfuming the neighborhood. Punks flooded cheap neighborhoods like West Oakland. We lived everywhere that was poor because we were penniless—almost all the time. That was why our politics leaned far left. We lived in little societies that welcomed everyone, white, brown, black, Asian. Whoever wanted to be one of us could. All they needed was anger, and once you were in, we took care of one another. West Oakland, with all its warehouse space, was a prairie for punks—like we'd rode covered wagons from Kansas, hunkering down in abandoned buildings.

I wished my dad could see these dirty empires we built.

In one punk house, I had lived with a junkie who was an ordained minister and had a tattoo of a devil on his shoulder. He'd shoot crank and wander the hallways reciting Scripture, scratching at his devil tattoo like it was a rash. We even tried to take care of him, though he was immune to help.

Trick and I hoofed toward the bay, past the stolen cars, the homeless encampments. The march to change the whole hood hadn't gotten to this stretch yet. Shanties of tarps and tents and shopping carts. Wrecked RVs like prehistoric skeletons. And the unmistakable stink of burning tinfoil to toast your tar heroin or crack.

We were about to walk under 880; the highway above us barked, keened, shook. It was like we were in a house and the roof was coming down. The more we walked into the tunnel, the darker it got.

"Okay," she said, "can you learn all these songs in one day or not?"

"We knocked out the first in fifteen minutes. We're good."

"You play way better than Got Jokes."

"No comment."

"He plays like he got his first period," she said.

"He plays like Green Day."

"Fuck Green Day," she said.

If there was a wedding chapel in West Oakland, I'd throw her over my shoulder and march there singing "All Night Long" by One Man Army. Steal a car after we were officially hitched, dangle those dumb soup cans off the back.

"I really dig your voice," I said.

We were almost out of the tunnel—almost to the light again.

"Got Jokes plays the guitar too clean. His whole sound has hand sanitizer all over it. I think your songs would sound better if I threw these parts in the mud, made 'em dirty. I know how to do right by your songs."

"I want a kick-ass guitarist," she said.

"I'll do my best."

It wasn't hard for me to admit that her songs were better than mine. I was a good guitarist and an okay throat, if nobody else in the room could sing—but Trick had a charisma that could give the stars in the Norwegian night a run for their money.

"And you're not some savior saving my band," she said. "I'm the only savior we need, asshole."

"I agree with you."

"I know who I am."

"Everyone is gonna know who you are," I said.

"Change his guitar parts. Give them balls. If it sounds better, we'll do it tonight. Best idea wins."

"You don't care how your old man feels about me changing his parts?"

"This isn't about feelings," she said. "It's about All the Fuss."

Once out of the tunnel, there was a laundromat with its security gate down, even though it was midday. There was, say, a three-foot gap between the gate and the front door, and in that space, there was a man on the ground, trapped.

"Boy, it's been a day," he said to us.

Trick started laughing, walked up to his bars. I felt like a prison guard in that moment, like I had all the power. "Who locked you in there?" she asked him.

"My sister. This is our business. She locked me in here to think."

"Do you deserve it?" Trick asked.

"Are you asking from my perspective or my sister's?"

"I'm asking for the truth," Trick said, and somewhere my father's ghost whispered in my ear: *She's a seeker, too.*

"And that old saw that it takes two to tango does not apply here," the man said about his sister. "This is a hundred percent my mess." He put his hand through the security gate at an awkward angle for a shake.

We both shook his hand.

"How long you been in there?" Trick asked.

"Since about noon."

"That's not so bad," Trick said.

"If you see her, tell her I'm ready to apologize."

"Has she locked you in here before?"

"Two other times."

"Did you deserve those, too?" Trick said.

"Oh, of course. My sister might be harsh, but she's fair," he said.

"Do you want water?" I asked him.

"Yes! Thank you."

"I don't have any on me," I said, "but I can go get some."

"That's disappointing," he said, falling glum. "Why word it like that if you don't have any on you? Now all I can think about is how thirsty I am."

I wanted to cheer him up and patted my pockets, found half a pack of beef jerky.

"Won't the salt make me even thirstier?" he asked.

He had a point.

But he put his hand through the bars anyway, and I handed him the jerky.

"Do you want us to break you out?" I asked.

"First, you give me beef jerky, and now, you're offering to spring me! You're nice."

"Not really," I said.

"I think so," he said, "but leave me in here. I'd just have to pay for the damage. It's easier to pay this way. I love that you offered." He bit off a hunk of jerky, chewing and talking. "She'll let me out soon and say I must close the store tonight, sleep here, give her space."

"At least you two have a system," Trick said.

"I'm getting sad again, thinking about hurting her feelings," he said.

I remembered how much I had enjoyed hearing Amy sing in the shower, and that triggered an idea. I pointed at Trick and said to our new friend, "She is a singer. Maybe if you ask real nice, she'll sing to you."

"That would be swell," he said.

"Is that it?" Trick said. "That's how you're asking real nice?"

"I was answering him," he said, pointing at me. "I was about to address you directly, miss. It would've sounded like this: It would be my honor if you'd consider singing me a song."

That was exactly what she did, a cappella, belting out Bikini Kill's "Double Dare Ya." She growled and ran her fingers on his bars to keep the beat. She even had stage presence performing in front of a laundromat to a lousy brother.

I tried not to watch her, as she was doing this for him, and I wasn't really a part of it—so instead, I watched her by watching him, his delighted face, his stained-glass window, his medical marijuana, his kaleidoscope, his MRI machine, his playground, his hot-air balloon, his bagpipes, his emotional support animal, his twelve-step day care, his hot yoga, his recycling plant, his protective eyewear, his myths.

Look at it from his perspective: One minute you are behind bars, feeling sorry for yourself, all alone, and the next you witness a miracle, a man handing you some beef jerky, an unhinged angel sidling up to your cage, firing up her furious pipes.

ᛈ

Trick and I kept on our scenic trek. On the next corner, in a vacant lot, there was a gigantic brown teddy bear plopped there. I mean, this stuffed animal was twenty feet high. I'd never seen anything like it.

We stopped, gawked at it like it was the northern lights.

"Please tell me," she said, "that you see that colossal bear, too."

"Don't worry. It's real."

This unbelievable animal reminded me of a trip to Hollywood Boulevard with some old friends from a punk house, and we were on acid and speed and whiskey, and we steered our longship down there at a hundred miles per hour—and once we got there, we peeped a man in a Wolverine costume on the sidewalk right when we got out of the car. I liked those old X-Men comics, because the real Wolverine acted like a Viking, and I asked this fake Wolverine from Hollywood to take a picture with me and I put my arm around him and smiled. I was high and happy, this was me and Wolverine, being chums, a couple of knuckleheads, and he even asked if we had any extra LSD to share, which made me laugh, a superhero asking for acid, and I slipped him a couple of tabs, told him it was on the house, thanking him for all he had done to keep humankind safe from monsters—and a couple weeks later, I looked at the picture, and Wolverine had an erection, right there on Hollywood Boulevard, right there in his uniform, right there in my picture, and I thought, *We will do anything in this life to feel less alone.*

Now I motioned to the huge teddy bear in the vacant lot, said to Trick, "Someone sodomized that bear."

"This wasn't a one sodomizer kind of situation," she said. "Nah, we're talking a full-on teddy bear gang bang."

Then we stared at it for a few more seconds, imagining appalling pornographic images.

Then she had another idea.

ᚠ

She took the front; I took the back. It seemed like the gentlemanly end to take in case there had been any bear penetration. It probably weighed seventy-five pounds, not too heavy but awkward, passive weight.

I was having fun. Nothing smelled like wastewater. Not even a violated bear could bring down my mood. I wasn't even thinking about Dusty running off to Wes. No, I'd just heard Trick sing.

"What happened to your eye?" she said as we staggered with the stuffed animal.

"I gave it to Jesse."

"I wouldn't piss on him if he was on fire," she said.

"I know—but I was worse than him before I got clean."

"But *why'd* you give him your eye?"

"I walked in his place ready to put a beating on him, but he was gonna kill himself with a razor. And I happened to . . . walk in . . . right then. I saved him. Felt like it meant something. So I took out my eye and told him it was a pill that could heal him."

"You said that?"

"The eye actually is lucky."

"And he ate it," she said. "That's messed up."

A man drove by, honking, yelling, "There's a bear on the loose! I'll radio animal control!"

For a minute, we were like a couple, carrying a couch to their place, buying furniture to fix it up. We were on a Sunday jaunt to Ikea or Crate & Barrel. We were normies. We had insurance cards and airbags. We got acupuncture.

"I'm sorry about your gear getting stolen," I said.

"You're getting it back, right?"

"I will."

"Then who cares?" she said. "This way, we get to gig together tonight."

"Two gigs, if you count the laundromat."

We lugged the teddy bear back to Sound Check's parking lot, past Amy and Jesse, dragged it inside and into my studio, planted it in the hole, long way, the bear lying down on its back, but basically forming a whole, probably-got-sodomized wall. Now our bands had their own rooms again, though who knew where things would stand with Dusty and me when all this shook out.

Trick and I stood looking at the big bear. We were sweating and laughing. We were alone. She grabbed me by the biceps, kissed me, looked at my eye patch. "Are you really a porn star?" she asked.

"Lower your expectations," I said.

"You're kinda scary." She kissed me again.

"So are you," I said.

"Hey," Got Jokes said from the other side of the bear, "are you hooking up? What about me, man?!"

Þ

I came out front of the studio to Jesse and Amy. I unlocked the maroon and now war-torn 1886 Reliant and got into the passenger side.

"Lock it," said Jesse, "fast. Trick's going to kill me."

"You'll certainly need to make amends there," I said, "but cheer up, once the gear is back, she'll relax."

But was that true? You never knew with a Valkyrie.

Jesse put his hand over his mouth and opened his door, puking in the parking lot again.

Amy and I shared a moment of eye contact, and then she said, "Being a nurse to a junkie is like taking care of a puppy. Except puppies are cute, so you don't care about all the fluids you're swabbing up."

"Thanks for helping him."

Jesse retched again, then pulled himself back in the Reliant and passed out on her shoulder.

"This is as close as I've ever gotten to motherhood," she said, and we both laughed. "I don't mind watching him. It actually feels sort of good to help. Don't tell him, but I like it."

"It does feel good to help."

"I didn't expect it," she said, "but yeah."

I was right about Amy, about what I saw in her eyes when we first met. I knew she was capable of being more than a crook. The world had plenty of those. I handed her the keys to the Reliant. "My advice is to stay on the road," I said, "or go to a friend's house where Wes can't find you."

"I don't want to bring any of my friends into my mess," she said.

"I'll settle all this with Wes soon. I'll call you once I know what's what."

She shook the keys back and forth. "One thing," she said, "if I keep him in the car, he's definitely going to yack in it."

"That's okay," I said. "It's Got Jokes's ride."

# 7

"A BROWN BEAR," my father said, shaking me from sleep, "he is who you fight today."

We always woke at four to work out.

"Let the others rot in the rack," Tron told me, "while we attack this day on a bloodthirsty quest for joy. They rest; we train. We get better here in this life, and they only improve in their dreams. We'll outwork the world, boy, I'll teach you. That's what I do. It's who I am. You'll be the same."

Glima: the martial art of the Viking. Hand to hand. Wrestling. Techniques these days most associated with judo and jiujitsu. And weapons: sword, spear, ax. We started every day of the week with combat drills and simulations, beginning with calisthenics, pull-ups and chin-ups on a tree branch, push-ups in the dirt, handstand push-ups against the studio, finishing with animal crawls. This last one was where you walked on four limbs, bringing your back down close to the ground, moving like a wolf. He made me do this up and down hills, made me do this for hours, days, months. At first, my hands got gnarled, bruised, lost nails, infected gashes. But after a year, my hands turned into paws, callused and limber, quick with crazy grip strength. I had no feelings in my hands, and that was one of the traits that made me so gifted with my fists.

"Our forefathers fought in this rough country," my father said, prepping me for our winter workouts. "We have snow and ice most of the year, and we use our surroundings as an advantage. We don't get cold. We can't. Impossible." We did push-ups on the ice. I did my sit-ups on the ice with no shirt on while he kicked me in the ribs. We wrestled on the snow in our drawers.

And, of course, those animal crawls kept being a daily part—hard in the snow, you never knew what was beneath the surface. But I learned to read nature. It became my favorite time of our days, these animal crawls; they were how we got to know each other, prowling, curious wolves.

My father led by example. He never asked me to do anything that he wasn't doing as well. We were a father-son pack, traveling the hills of our ancestors. The closer I kept my face to the land the more I could hear ghosts—they weren't dead, weren't defeated; they still lived in the soil.

On one of those four-legged adventures after the spring thaw, he said to me, "Okay, here is today's question."

We were in the grass around a lake. The earth got softer as I crept to the water's edge. There was a birch tree, its leaves mottling the ground with shade. The mud stunk like leeks.

He went on. "I want to ask about me. I've put this off, but I wonder. All these years, never meeting. When you imagined me, what was I like in your head?"

"Mom said you looked like Iggy Pop, except giant, so I kind of pretended like Big Iggy was my dad."

"Your mother was the first person to play me the Stooges."

"Me, too," I said, and we laughed while we crawled along the riverbank. "I tried not to think of you, to be honest. If I did, it was mostly to hate you."

"Because I wasn't there?"

"Because you were missing it," I said.

"Missing what?"

"We could have had a family," I said, "and we'll never know now."

We crawled in the tall grass for a few seconds, the only noises the lapping water, the insects. I smelled something rotting, turned up the hill, and soon our noses found a dead puffin.

Our snouts were close to the sour bird.

"We ate these," my father said.

"We did?"

"Our ancestors used ropes and swung down massive cliffs to get the puffins' eggs. They were delicacies."

"But we're not eating this dead one, right?"

My father howled, shook his head, then led us back toward home. "We are a family now," he said, "and to that end, we need to up your training."

"How?"

My father and I had been sparring glima, so I could feel the weight and strength of a grown man. He made me bleed. To my father, there was no way to simulate the stakes of real bare-knuckle violence between family. He got me as far as he could on his own, and now it was time to turn up the heat, to see what I was made of, so every week, a new boy, one whose father was like Tron, raising his kin in the traditions of the brutal Old World, with Norse power.

I fought Toke.

I fought Ulf.

I fought Knud.

I fought Harald.

I fought Trygve.

I fought Gorm.

I fought all three brothers in the Johansen family.

I fought two more from the Larsens.

I fought Frod and Sten and Erik and Bjorn and Bo and Arne and Leif and Kare and Skarde and Skarde again and Skarde a third time, the tough son of a bitch. And now we were back to where we started: my father rousing me from the rack, saying it was time to fight the brown bear.

I knew he was half mad on a good day, but I also knew that the other half of him was talent. You stood in the studio, watching him curve these glass birds into life, creating the illusion of motion, intention. The birds didn't look still—they looked *frozen* in flight, soaring at speed.

Around home, he talked to no one but me and his birds. He worked all night in manic fits, often for days at a time, and I'd wake and hear him in mid-monologue, talking to a dead elder or a glass bird: "You make art and it's a limb of you, making it is a form of self-amputation, that's what an artist risks in the reckless act of creation, we give it our imagination and attention, we make it beautiful, and we love it, and we love it—but we hack it off to a bloody stump and we hold the pulpy thing up and sell it for profit and maybe buy a nice jacket, and soon you can't even remember what that art looked like—that piece of your body that meant so much, it's a ghost, and you're just this disappearing mutilator with a new coat."

That morning I met the bear, the man approached our cabin in an old truck, a cage on its back with the two-year-old animal. The man said to my father, "It is an honor to be here with you. My family, we are big fans," and my father said, "You are welcome here for as many potato wines as you can consume," and they shook hands.

My father coached me a bit before they let the bear out. Same principles with the under- and overhooks. Same goal to lace your fingers behind the neck, squeezing your hands together, pulling down and controlling the position with weight and angles. Get to the ground. Dominate.

"But don't hurt the bear," my father said. "I mean, hurt it. But don't . . . *hurt* it."

"Should I choke it instead?"

"Don't hurt it."

"Okay."

"This is a bear," my father said.

"I know."

"And you are ready to fight this bear."

"I am, yes."

"So if it's a bear, and you're willing to fight it, what does that make you?"

"I'm a Viking, Father," I said.

"Tron."

"I'm a Viking, Tron."

We ran at each other, the bear and me. I locked my paws behind his neck, and he did the same. We jockeyed for position. We shucked each other from side to side. His power was unlike anything I'd ever felt, and he lunged forward and toppled me backward, and he fell on top of me, but too high, on my chest instead of near my waist to keep his balance on top, and I was able to buck him off, was able to scramble and take the bear's back, was able to put it in a rear naked choke, which wasn't technically glima, but I didn't care about technicalities while wrestling a bear, but my father called for me to release the bear, and I did, and the bear leaped around and gave me a huge hug, and that was one thing I learned right then, a deep and meaningful respect for the manner in which bears handled losing.

They were good sports, these bears.

Or this bear.

Maybe the rest of them were poor losers.

How would I know?

He and I became training partners.

ᚦ

"He's crying," Trick said as soon as I came back in the studio. She sat at the drum set. Her foot kept anxious sixteenth notes on the hi-hat.

"No, I'm not," Got Jokes said from the other side of the stuffed bear wall.

"He's saying he's not going to gig tonight with us," she said to me. "He's saying it's too humiliating."

I asked her if I should go talk to him.

"That's the last thing I want!" Got Jokes called. "I'm locking the door!"

She kept those sixteenth notes up, foot bouncing on the hi-hat pedal. "Might as well try," she said to me.

We heard him flip the bolt.

Trick fumed, the tempo of her sixteenth notes increasing.

I went to the bear wall and muscled a stuffed leg aside, so I could shimmy to Got Jokes. "Stay back!" he said, hopping up on the couch, like he was hiding from a mouse. I felt bad for Got Jokes. I didn't want or expect any of this to happen. He was the one who knocked on my door that morning, inviting me to be a part of this. So I understood why he'd want to back out of the gig. It wasn't easy for him to have to listen to Trick kiss me. Men had egos more fragile than one of my father's glass birds.

I'd give Got Jokes a gentle nudge to do the right thing here. We all need some help every so often. I was confident that I could coolly suggest the proper decision so he could rise to the occasion. "You're playing the goddamn gig!" I said, gentle nudging.

"What? No. Why?"

"For Trick. For yourself. You told me this is your big break. Don't let a dustup with me spoil that. This is Jawbreaker. These are your songs. Do right by the band."

He was starting to cry again. "Do you realize that you're the worst thing that's ever happened to me?" he asked. "You broke my hand, are playing guitar in my band tonight, and you're stealing my girl."

"So far."

"What?"

"I'm saying that yes, so far, those might seem like the worst things."

"No, man, I'm saying *you're* the worst thing."

"They're not the worst things," I said. "Not even close."

"That sounds like you're threatening me. Is that what's happening?"

"There are worse things."

"The emasculation continues," Got Jokes said.

I walked over to the bear, pushed its leg out of the way. "Come on. Let's all practice together." I held the stuffed leg open for him, showing that manners mattered, that we should be kind to each other, that we should let bygones lie in a graveyard and be friends, life was too short for grudges.

I wanted him to see that I could be gentle—that I wasn't solely piloted by my temper. I valued joy, too, and Got Jokes needed to know that. *I* needed to know that. Needed to remember that the world wasn't just made of real bears, though there were plenty of them out there, too. I had to hold on to the idea that there were stuffed ones, too.

I still held the leg; Got Jokes was thinking about what to do.

"After you," I said to him.

If anyone needed a little special attention, it was him. A man could only tow so much shame.

He sighed, wiped his eyes, saying, "I should've never knocked on your door," disappearing around the stuffed animal's bent leg.

And wasn't that one of the most confounding aspects of being alive—how we could endure the same system of events and extract different meanings? Yes, Got Jokes was right that since he knocked, he'd been ravaged in a hurricane of unwanted outcomes. And yet, for me, this was turning out to be one of the best days of my life. All this joy lifted me off the ground—I was weightless and flying, and one of my father's glass birds floated by, cawing, singing to me.

Þ

A couple hours later, my calm waters were abruptly disturbed.

A tweaker busted into the practice room holding a sawed-off shotgun, asking, "Who wants to take a ride?"

Shaved head, six feet, weighing a buck fifty or so. All bones. Hugging him would be like slow dancing with a sleeping bag full of spatulas.

I was over in the corner of the room, changing the record, dropping the needle on a Stiff Little Fingers seven-inch, the guitar barking the opening riff of "Suspect Device."

Got Jokes was on the floor, leaning against the couch.

Trick Wilma sat at the drum kit, guzzling water. The drummer who had no name or face had to give her roommate a ride and would be back in fifteen.

My machete was all the way across the room, leaning against the wall. My hitter-quitter was still tucked in the back of my pants, though no one would know that until the time was right.

We'd been practicing all their songs. They were sounding solid, and I rewrote almost all the guitar parts, a further embarrassment for poor Got Jokes. Still, he seemed to dig the songs better, and an hour into the breakneck rehearsal, we were all getting along, laughing, nodding, knowing the tracks were getting sick. I couldn't take my eye off Trick, listening to her screams, her madness, and I indulged in a fantasy that this music was our future.

That was when we decided to take a break so the drummer could give her friend a lift.

That was when I threw that SLF record on the turntable.

That was when the tweaker rampaged in—and now, there was his shotgun to consider.

"Who are you?" Trick said to him.

"This is a private session, sir," Got Jokes added.

Which made the tweaker laugh, and he said back, "Shhh. You might think I'm telling you to be quiet, but I'm only starting the word *shhhh-hhotgun*, which translates in your native tongue as 'shut the fuck up.'"

"She asked who you are," I said, moving to take the needle off the record.

"No! Leave it on," he said. "I love this song."

He sang along to the verse, bopping his head, then turned his attention back to Trick. "I work for Wes—and he's unhappy."

"Who the fuck is Wes?" Trick asked.

"You've got a big fucking mouth," he said to her.

I marched toward him, and he pointed the shotgun at my face. It was impossible for me to be afraid of a speed freak, even one brandishing something that could cut me in half. That wasn't to say tweakers weren't deadly. Of course they were. Tweakers were weasels, greedy and cunning and murderous, coated in slime and lies. And in their horrible junkie tunnel vision, they were insanely resourceful. I'd watched one make a glass pipe from a broken light bulb. I knew another with a steady habit who stole portable ATMs by putting a chain around them and connecting them to the back of his motorcycle, dragging them off, a wrecking ball for a tail.

This tweaker knew violence; anyone could see that. And still, it was impossible for me to be afraid, because I had longships gliding through my blood, and after years wrestling and growing up with that bear, a bag of spatulas was not a true adversary.

"You must be the guy who emailed Wes," he said to me. "You sure stirred up some havoc."

"Are you with Dusty?" I said. "Is he here, too? I'd like to talk to him."

"Dusty doesn't come on jobs like this."

"Jobs like what?"

"You'll fucking see," he said.

He mouthed another couple lines from the SLF song, made a point to smile at each of us. He noted the machete leaning against the wall behind him, and then he made a critical mistake.

He pointed at the machete. "Dusty also said you had a hitter-quitter," he said, "and warned me against letting you bring it along. That stays here."

Assumptions—they could destroy us.

# 8

MY FAVORITE THING to do was watch my father blow the glass. He was an industry, sweaty and defiant, towering over his work. He'd walk me through the various processes in his studio, hot and humid, and the part that excited me the most was when he'd use the blowpipe, sending puffs of air to contort the hot glass into any shape he wanted. He was ambitious, inspired to forge the art that only he could. The gods must've felt the same way, making life from nothing, stocking our planet with the peculiar: This was a platypus, and this was a dumbo octopus, and this was a goblin shark, and this was a pink fairy armadillo, and this was a capybara, and this scared, self-centered savage was called a human.

My father never made me feel like I was in the way or bothering him. I didn't think much about my mom, but when I did, my memories were mostly negative. I was a nuisance. I was always keeping her from doing what she really wanted to do. Tron never left ten dollars under a magnet on our refrigerator so I could order a pizza, so he could disappear on drunken quests for days at a time. No, Tron included me in his hobby, the birds, while my mother hated how I inconvenienced her boozing.

On this particular day, my father opened a locked cabinet near the back of his studio. There were a couple of big cardboard boxes on the bottom shelf, obscured behind cleaning supplies. He cleared away the clutter, then carried one out to the salvage yard, and I hauled the other.

The boxes were heavier than they looked. Once we plopped them down on the grass, he said to me, "Here is today's question: What will you do when you're not fighting?"

There was a chill in the air. After a couple months in the grass, it was almost ice season again—that was how Tron had described the Norwegian seasons to me when I first got there: two months of grass, ten of freeze.

"I don't know what I'll do," I said.

"Balance. We need quiet in our lives to complement the Viking madness. I have my glass birds—but what are you going to focus on?"

"I don't know."

He opened the box he'd carted, but I couldn't see what was inside. "What about learning a musical instrument?" He pulled out a long, skinny tube that looked like a frozen snake. "Our ancestors played this. A flute that was carved from bone."

"People bones?!"

"I'm sure that happened, too," he said, "but usually, they used animal shins." Tron brought the instrument to his mouth, blew a few notes.

"A people flute," I said, and it was a stunning visual in my boy brain: A Viking on the field of battle, killing an enemy, severing the leg at the knee, carving meat from the calf until it was just bone, then hollowing it out, licking his lips, gathering a deep breath, and right there, surrounded by war, he'd blow into his people flute. A quiet, almost fragile sound that required an immense amount of violence to create.

Tron laid the flute on the grass, reached into the box, pulled out a cow horn. "They also made instruments from these."

That made me laugh. "Playing a cow horn."

"Blew into the small end, and the call projected all over the village. That was how the men knew when it was time to go to war. A different kind of music."

Tron took a deep huff and lit the horn up. I wondered if the dead Vikings heard it from Valhalla and reached for an ax on instinct, before remembering their days on earth were over.

"I don't like that one," I said.

"They also played the lyre."

"What's that?"

He pulled a lyre out of the box, plucked a few strings. "A kind of harp."

"Was that made of bone, too?"

"In a sense. The strings were animal sinew. But their bodies were wood." He ran his fingers over the harp's strings a few more times, then grimaced at me. "This sounds like an old lady giving a lecture," he said, laying the lyre down in the grass, next to the flute and the cow horn.

Now Tron reached into the other box, the one I'd carried, and pulled out a huge wooden drum. No wonder it was so heavy.

"And they pounded drums, boy," he said. "Vikings knew how to make the dirt shudder." Tron let his hands loose on the drum, pounding, hard, slow, up and down. "Try it," he said to me, and so I hit it with him, father and son, drumming.

After a minute or so, we stopped. We were both a little winded but smiled at each other. He leaned over and kissed me on the cheek. It was the first time he'd ever done that. It was also the last.

"Should I learn how to play the drums?" I asked him.

"Did you like doing that?"

"I did."

"But you didn't love it."

"I loved doing it with you," I said.

"That's good. But we want this to be something you love doing by yourself, too. It is your quiet time."

"Okay. Then I don't want to play the drums."

"When you used to listen to Iggy with your mom, what instrument was your favorite?"

I didn't need to think about it at all. "The electric guitar!"

"What do you like about the electric guitar?"

"It sounds like a happy monster."

"It sounds like a happy monster," Tron echoed, smiling at me. "I like that. And this is a happy monster, too."

"What is?"

"This coincidence. Wait here." Tron split back into his studio, and I studied the instruments lined up on the grass: the flute, the cow horn, the drum. The music of the warrior. I wondered how it sounded when they sang. I bet the Valkyries did most of it. I bet it brought you to your knees, hearing a Valkyrie scream a war song at you.

Tron came back outside wearing an electric guitar. "Iggy's real name was James, and that's why your mom insisted it was yours, too."

"I know."

"I know you know," he said, "but let me finish."

"Okay."

"If you're named after him, and you think the guitar in his band sounds like a happy monster, it only seems right that you play one, too."

"Where did you get that?"

"I made a glass bird for Keith Richards. He gave me this Telecaster as payment."

Tron walked up to me, took the guitar off, and threaded it around my neck. I held the happy monster, having no idea what to do with it—but somehow knowing that I was never supposed to take it off for the rest of my life. I had a phantom limb that I didn't even know about. And somebody just returned it.

ᛈ

It was the late afternoon now, and we stood at a Cadillac, the tweaker with the shotgun behind the three of us: Trick, Got Jokes, and me.

Maybe when you heard the word *Cadillac* you imagined something classic. No, this Caddy came straight from Helheim, roared out of the underworld burning worn-down rubber. It was so broken, so uncared for, so rusted out, that its engine bong-hit coughed, and it shuddered like a vibrating bed.

The tweaker put Trick and me in the back seat, then he climbed in next to us, right behind the passenger seat, where Got Jokes plopped. Nobody was worried about him. There was a bruiser in the driver's seat. My size. He wore a woman's stocking over his head, so I couldn't see what kind of fire he had in his eyes. Muscles didn't really matter in a fight. The outcome of a battle was always in the stare. It told you right away what a person was willing to endure to win. To survive.

He also had on a bulky jacket, so I couldn't tell what weapons he had on him. I had to assume a gun. A blade at least.

I would need to get to him fast.

That was what glima was all about. Glima, from the Norse word *glimt*, which meant "flash." That meant the glima fights were quick bursts of brutal technique. Vikings were the Navy SEALs of their day. You wrestled, tossed, or tripped your opponent to the ground. Used a sword, ax, or knife to end him. Your shield, your hands, your forehead if you had to.

I was getting an old feeling. Not joy. Big bees of nerves swirled in unified flight through me. You were scared before a scrap, and anyone who said differently was a posturing coward.

A warrior knew how to shape that alarm into a spear.

A real barbarian fought better because of the fear.

I already told you that my hitter-quitter was a foot of pipe, but I didn't mention that I'd filed one end down, arrow sharp. It could be used as a knife, swung like a sword, wielded like an ax at close range.

The tweaker said to his big friend, "Drive fast and recklessly. Let's give them one last adventure."

ᚹ

I found my father doing the same thing he had done on the day I arrived: He was in jeans, shirtless, burning a stack of pages in an oil drum. Flecks of paper traveled up from the fire to the sky, messages defying gravity.

I had just woken up. He had woken me up. Banging on the side of the oil drum. Burning pages. He argued with his glass birds: "I'll save us from the future," he told them. "I promise. We'll never be a commodity. Nobody will ever buy us at a cash register."

I watched for a minute from the doorway.

The sonorous fire.

His words.

He tore another page in half and threw it in the drum. Up it went, sparks, wisps of story: a scorched ghost.

"What are you burning?" I asked him.

"The same thing I burn every year."

"And what is that?"

"My memoir."

"What's a memoir?"

"A book about my life."

"Why burn a book about your life?"

"I've burned this book," he said, "every year for twenty years. I write it. I promise my publisher that I won't light it on fire this time. But then I do."

"That must make them upset."

"It does."

"Why do you do it?"

"I don't want to light it on fire. I like writing it. But every time, as I'm supposed to turn it in, I question my motives. Why tell them all the secrets about my glass birds? Why let anyone into my head? I can't bring myself to reduce the complexities of life to a coloring book."

"I don't understand."

"Books need readers—and that means books are meant to be discovered in the future. And I don't want to share our stories with the future. I make my birds to share them with the past, our past, boy. So I write my story down to honor our bloodline, our country, my birds. But if it becomes a book, it's for the future—and I want to talk only backward in time. The people who have already lived matter so much more to me than those who come next. That's what nobody knows about my birds. They travel in time, back to the Viking age. Backward in time, my birds."

"Okay, Tron."

My father's brain was filled with too many birds chirping, so he couldn't organize his thoughts, and the ones he could make out had been mangled, every syllable warped to silly perspectives.

"Would you like to burn more of the story?" he asked me.

I nodded, and he handed me a chapter. "Is this a good part?"

"It is," he said, "so throw it in the fire."

I followed his command. We watched that good part of his memoir singe in the blaze, get cremated, its smoky spirit moving into the sky. I wanted to read everything, wanted to know the whole story, this whole man, an artist, a mystery, a pyro.

Please just give me one page to read.

Please let me know as much about you as I could.

Please.

"Watch the sparks carry off paragraphs to fly with my birds," he said. "These sparks—these are the lights that take us away."

I threw a few more pages in the fire. "Where do they take us?"

"Where does what take you?"

"The lights."

"What lights?" Tron asked, looking skyward.

"The sparks—you said they are the lights that take us away. To where?"

"To Quiet."

"Quiet? That's the name of the place?"

"It is one of its names, yes," he said.

"And what happens when we get there, Father?"

"Tron."

"What happens when we get there, Tron?"

"We dance. We get to dance forever."

"I don't know how to dance."

"Fighters are usually great dancers. All the footwork. On your toes. I'll teach you soon."

"We get to Quiet, and we dance," I said.

"Yes," he said, "that's where the lights take us. And you—I don't need to write anything down anymore because I'm going to teach it all to you. You'll be my book, boy."

I continued to shovel pages in the fire. "I will?"

"You'll have great adventures."

"Yeah?"

"When the call comes, you'll fight. You'll protect what matters, won't you?"

"I'll try . . . Tron."

"Here," he said, handing me another bundle, "this is my favorite part of the book, and I'd like you to annihilate it for me."

"Can I read it first?"

"No."

"Why?"

"If I wanted people to read it, I wouldn't be setting it on fire. Sparks are just particles—of our books, of our bodies—as we float to Valhalla. Don't worry, boy, we'll see the book when we get there."

"I can't read a page?"

"I've burned the book all the other years. I want you to do it this time."

He wasn't going to answer me, to hear me, to listen. He wouldn't or couldn't. I wanted so badly to read a page, but I wanted even more to stay in his good graces. So I pitched it into the flames.

While we watched it burn, he said, "Make your adventures loud and bloody. You're the book now. Be the book."

ᚦ

The big guy obliged the tweaker's request to drive fast and recklessly, and we took off down Grand. Since this part of town was mostly industrial during the day, we weaved fast around the neighborhood, blowing stop signs and red lights. We sped by a mural depicting hairy brown lines, a large system of sprawling roots. Three words ran across the top: WE RUN DEEP—but on the outside of the building, there was a FOR SALE sign.

The tweaker said, while clutching his shotgun close to his chest but pointing it at me, "Wes is rejecting your proposal and refusing to meet you. His counter is simple: His relationship with Toby and Amy will continue. We're going to beat you near death. Broken bones. Compound fractures. I'm even gonna knock out your teeth with the barrel of my gun."

Got Jokes had his head bent down, trying to vanish from sight. He whispered to the tweaker, "Sir, I've already suffered an injury today, and I'm what's called an innocent bystander in this situation."

The tweaker took his eyes off me, just for a second, and I slowly moved my hand to grip the hitter-quitter hidden in the back of my pants. Now he brought his attention back to me, pumped the shotgun, inched it close to my face again.

"Everything goes back to how it's supposed to be," the tweaker said to me. "Wes and Amy. So you heal up from the bad day you're about to have, and you fuck off. If I see you again, I'll kill you."

The hitter-quitter came from nowhere, knocking the barrel of his gun up.

A shot ringing, busting through the roof of this Helheim ride.

Our ears ringing, ringing.

Me swinging, swinging the hitter-quitter like an ax, splitting the tweaker's forehead.

Gushing, whimpering.

Clutching his wound.

The big guy roasted the Caddy's brakes, and we started to skid to a stop—but I had about five seconds until he could take his hands off the wheel.

Five seconds to enjoy myself with the tweaker.

His hands were still up by his forehead, too high to protect his throat.

I punched his Adam's apple. I boxed his ears. I grabbed his hair and slammed his head into my elbow, blood spraying all over the back seat, all over Trick and me.

The car finally stopped.

The big guy turned around now, but he was too slow, too late, and that cute little stocking on his head wasn't going to be much of a cushion.

Me bouncing the hitter-quitter off the big guy's temple.

Once.

Twice.

Not too hard.

I wasn't going to kill anyone.

Not again.

Just one last shot from the hitter on him for good measure, the softest of the three-piece. Just a little kiss telling him that I didn't dig the way he drove.

I climbed over the seat, wedged myself between the big guy and Got Jokes, and I took that sharpened edge of the hitter-quitter, and I planted it right in his thigh, a half inch from his femoral artery.

The big guy yelped, and I slammed his head into the driver's-side window, red bubbles frothing from his mouth, and because of the stocking over his face, the blood in there squished around, up and down and toward his cheeks, almost a symmetrical pattern, a Rorschach test. And if someone asked me what I saw in the blood blot, I would tell them the truth: I saw Trick onstage, screaming her head off, an ocean of fans stretching so far that they made their own horizon—so many of them swarming into the distance that they showed you Earth was round.

"I'm right by your artery," I said to him. "I move it half an inch, you'll bleed out."

"Please," he said.

"Hit his artery," Trick said. "He deserves it."

In a past life, she would've cut your head off with an ax, then sipped potato wine like it was nothing. I could imagine us on the battlefield, killing and thrilled with bloodlust. And once our work was done in combat, we danced right there, humming our favorite punk songs with her head on my shoulder, swaying with the dead scattered around us.

That image of us inspired me to pour it on some with the big guy, see how much I could scare him into cooperating. I put a bit more pressure on the hitter-quitter in his thigh, and he writhed in pain.

"Or I could pull this out of you and use it to spill your intestines with one slice across your belly," I said to him. "I could pull them all out of you and wear them around my neck like leis."

"Aloha," Trick said, "but gross."

"Sorry," I said.

"Jesus," he said, "what do you want to know?!"

# WHOLE FOODS HALLUCINATION

**KNOW THIS MAN** from somewhere. Short, a bike chain worn like a choker around his neck, a shirt of the hard-core band the Dirty Vanirs underneath his black Whole Foods apron.

He's skinny, with a round and cherubic face, straight black hair pomaded to points and angles, rehab chic.

He's the checker.

I'm in his line.

And I don't know how I got here.

The next customer, the one right before me, unloads her basket of artisan eighty-dollar candles made from the blubber of extinct super walruses. She gives Billie a double take, then says to him, "Excuse me, are you—"

"Am I," Billie affirms, "the guy who's never been employee of the month, even though I have all the tangible accomplishments of one— and some might say I also possess all the intangibles, too? Are you asking if that's me? If so, then yes. I am that spurned, non–employee of the month."

He rolls the candles, one by one, across his scanner, chirping artisan commerce, sounding like laughter. Billie shakes his head and mutters under his breath.

"Right," the candle customer says, "okay—but aren't you in a band?"

"Of course I'm in a band. We're all in bands. I've never been employee of the month there, either. Thanks for bringing that up."

"Haven't you won a Grammy?"

"Grammys."

"So why are you here?"

He puts her candles in her tote, along with a receipt, then points right at me. "I'm here for him."

The candle lady vanishes. She doesn't walk away. She disappears. Then I notice his name tag says BILLIE.

"Put your items on the conveyor belt, please," he says.

"I don't have any . . ." but suddenly, that isn't true. There's a full shopping cart in front of me, piled high with pickled fruit, plums from the look and size of them.

I hold a jar up to my eye. "What are these?"

"Those are songs."

So I hold a jar up to my ear instead. I unscrew the lid an inch—and I can hear it. Fast. Mean. Loud. Punk rock.

"This is good."

"That's you and Trick," he says, starting to scan the jars. "You'll write that song together."

"We will?"

"Next October."

"How do you know that?"

He keeps beeping these jars of songs over the scanner.

"It's a great song," says Billie. "You'll write a lot together."

"We will?"

"You're gonna get famous."

"Yeah, right," I said, laughing.

"What's so funny?"

"I don't want to like you," I say, "but I really do."

He scans the last jar, the last song. He holds it up to his ear like it's a conch shell, like he can hear the song, or hear the hearts who wrote it. I watch Billie listening to a song that supposedly I'll go on to write in the future. I watch him smile and bob his head to the beat.

"This is your hit," he says. "Would you like to hear it?"

# PART 2

## GARBAGE STARS

# 9

I F YOU'D NEVER BEEN IN, it would be like an astronaut trying to explain the customs of an alien planet. Who you were the minute before they caged you up, none of that mattered. You did nauseating acts; it was the only way to come through. Even you, with your enlightened, levelheaded mind, your mutual funds and IRAs, your thicket of impossible, brazen assumptions about the future—all that rotted instantaneously in Quentin. You learned on the quick what you were capable of doing. No reason to judge convicts on their transgressions. Just thank your gods that you didn't have to make those same decisions, because they weren't decisions at all.

Not really.

Not if you ever wanted to walk back out.

And hopefully, you still had a seed of a person in you on the other side.

Denis, a cellie of mine for a few months, was a diaper sniper. This made his time a nightmare. Denis had to masturbate in front of a CO for extra protection, and still he took gruesome beatings, always out-muscled, outmanned. But I wasn't about to tell you some cable TV *Jurassic Park* bullshit around prison. No, this was a small, simple story about a human being named Denis who had been slowly going blind.

For years, he told me, he'd had glaucoma, everything losing color, focus. There were no foregrounds or backgrounds left for Denis. No, there were only walls of color, all oozing toward blackness.

Denis knew better than to wake me up early, but on that morning, he said to me before the sun was up, "Hey, can you help me?"

He'd turned on the little light, stood next to my bunk.

"I'm sleeping, Denis."

"I know. And I'm sorry."

"Let's talk later."

"The thing is," he said, "that I'm about to go blind."

I sat up in bed. "What?"

"Right now."

"Yell for a guard."

"It's all been getting dimmer and dimmer," he said, "but it's all almost gone, man. I can barely see."

"So go to the doc."

"Oh, believe me, I've seen plenty of them, and they all said this day would come sooner or later. I just didn't know today was the one."

"You started this by asking if I could help you."

"Right," Denis said, "I did say that. Sorry. I'm flustered. I've never gone blind before. It's a lot to take in. I want you to help me figure out what I should look at. What's the last thing I should see?"

We peered around. A toilet, a sink, bunks. A laundry line. Ratty towels. Books. Blank walls.

"You," he said.

"You want to see me?"

"I'd like to look at another person when I go blind," he said. "That seems nice."

What was I supposed to say? Was there a way to deny such an eroding request?

He'd never see this earth again, never know another sunset. A child. A fire. A narwhal. These things would all be conjectures. Or they'd be memories—at least he'd have those, though as we all knew those deformed with time, could disappear as our minds curdled.

I stood up, right in front of Denis. He was only about five feet ten, so he gazed up at me. Ten seconds of us staring, and then I asked, "What should we talk about?"

"Let's not," he said. "Let's just stare at each other."

Two men, two animals, two jewels in our chests, simply staring.

I had only one eye.

He had two but would soon have none that worked.

Nobody else alive knew what was at stake in that moment. No one knew that another human was losing a sense, and no one would have cared anyway. A convict. A piece of shit. Good. Served him right.

In one way or another, we all went blind.

"Okay," Denis said to me.

"Okay what?"

"That's it."

"You can't see me anymore?"

"The sun," said Denis, "set on the entire solar system."

ᛈ

"Now I see you!" said Hild once I walked back into the army supply store, straight after leaving the violence with the tweaker and the big guy, who were enjoying some trunk time in the Caddy. I left Trick and Got Jokes out there with the instructions to hit the horn if they needed me to pop out on the quick.

Nobody else was in the store, and she greeted me with that same lovely enthusiasm. She smiled, and it meant something to me immediately.

That drug again: joy.

In the Old World, the eighth rune in our alphabet was wunjo, a symbol of harmony and joy. The glyph looked like an angular, capital *P*. Simple and punk rock. Hild should be wearing wunjo on her shirt like it was a band's logo.

"I saw, maybe, sixty percent of you last time," she said.

"Sixty?"

"Fine," she said, "you got me. More like twenty percent."

"How do I look now?"

"Much bigger than I thought."

"Anything else?"

"I didn't realize you had a mohawk."

"Do you like it?"

"It suits you."

"What else?" I asked her.

"You're younger than I thought."

"How old did you think I was?"

"When I was blind, you put off the energy of somebody who's seen some shit," she said. "Usually, you got to be older to be like that."

"Anything else?"

"You chose a good eye patch."

"Thanks for giving it to me. And the machete, too."

"Are you kidding? You saved my blind ass. It was the least I could, giving you a machete. Now what brought you back to the store?"

"Blankets, handcuffs, duct tape."

"Now, Saint," she said, "you wouldn't throw a blanket party without me, right? That would hurt my feelings."

"No, ma'am."

She studied me for a beat, smiled again.

Maybe it was the violence from the car. Maybe it was adrenaline still kicking in me. But I started to wonder if she'd been right earlier, when she said I'd come into the store for a reason. I was either her little break or she was mine, or we were both our little breaks.

Was this what it felt like to have a mother?

I wondered regularly what mine would have looked like now. If she faked her death, say, and we bumped into each other on the street, would we know? I chose to believe we would, we'd have to, and then we'd re-acquaint ourselves with a long game of Did That Happen? and we'd tell each other our life stories through true or false questions, cooking up tall tales, regaling our lost family with the successes, building stories bigger than cities, and once we were comfortable together again, we'd confess the gutters of suffering we told no one about—

"Where did you go?" Hild said.

Oh, right.

She and I were having a conversation.

"Do you have children?" I asked.

She put her hands on her hips. "Are you planning on using the blankets, handcuffs, and duct tape on my kids?"

"Was it that obvious?"

She came around the counter and got a small shopping cart. Then she moved through the aisles, snatching the items I needed like a personal shopper. "I have a daughter who lives in Atlanta," she said, "and a dipshit boy in Detroit. And if my dipshit boy came into an army supply store buying blankets and handcuffs and duct tape, I'd like to think the person working there might ask a couple questions of him, making sure he knew what he was doing."

"Sure," I said, "that makes sense."

She stopped in front of the camping supplies, the blankets. "How many?" she said. "What color?"

"Ten, black."

Hild stacked the blankets in her arms, placed them gently in the cart, and we kept moving. "I'd hope the person working asked my dipshit kid the most important question."

"What's that?"

"Is it worth it?"

We walked toward the duct tape, rounded a corner that had a display of canteens and beer koozies. There was an American flag pinned up behind them.

"Are you sure you don't need a canteen?" she asked. "You got to stay hydrated."

"I'm good on canteens."

"'Is it worth it?' That's the first question. Here's the next: Whatever *it* is," she said, "sounds like it comes at a heavy cost. I always wonder— who decides that cost?"

We stopped in front of the duct tape.

"How many rolls?" she asked.

"Ten."

"A real tape enthusiast."

"I bet you're a good mom," I said.

She plucked ten rolls of duct tape and threw them in the cart. "That's not true at all. I was all-time bad."

She led me to the various wrist and hand restraints. We stopped in front of a wall of handcuffs.

"What kind of cuffs you in the market for?" she asked. "Kinky Kitty Cat or Old Johnny Law?"

"The latter, unfortunately."

"How many pairs?"

"Two."

"I thought you were going to say ten again."

"I thought about it. To mess with you."

She lobbed the handcuffs into the cart and moved everything to the register. I followed behind her.

"There's one extra question I hope he'd be asked," she said, ringing up and bagging the merchandise. "Do you mind one more?"

"Of course not."

"It's personal."

"That's fine."

She stepped toward me and looked in my eye with her clear ones, not a single bloodshot line left from earlier today. She wasn't smiling at all now, and she asked her tangled question: "Why do you think you need to pay such a heavy cost, what's the point of putting yourself in harm's way, why won't you protect yourself?"

These were good questions.

Or what she called "one more."

You didn't ask questions like these unless you cared about someone. And it was hard to care here. This world possessed such apathy toward us, and yet we all wanted to live, to stay here—we wanted to love.

Þ

Minutes later, we emerged from the storefront with Hild helping me carry all my shopping. She peered into the Caddy: In the passenger seat, Got Jokes, looking like he might piss himself. He hadn't said a word since the fracas.

In the driver's seat, there she was, Trick Wilma.

On the radio, the Kills sang "Pull a U."

"Should we load this in the trunk?" asked Hild.

"Let's just put it all in the back seat."

We'd done a pretty awful job of cleaning up all the blood, and Hild noticed, of course, but she didn't say anything about it.

Instead, she asked, "Who are your friends, Saint?"

I motioned to Trick: "This is Trick Wilma—the person I want you to meet."

Trick beamed at Hild, said, "Saint told me the story about how you two met earlier—it sounded real sweet." Then Trick's face soured. "Except for the pepper spray part. That must've hurt like a motherfucker."

"Oh, you two are good together, Saint," Hild said to me, patting me on the arm as she smiled at Trick.

"You have the wrong idea, lady," Got Jokes chirped from the passenger seat. "Trick's still *my* girlfriend."

Hild's skeptical gaze sunk Got Jokes farther into his seat.

"When will this day stop kicking me in the balls?" he asked.

Þ

We dropped Got Jokes off at Sound Check. He was going to load up the gear and get it to Gilman. We needed to drop off the guys at their

Alcatraz. They were duct-taped and flattened out in the trunk of the car. They had pieces of tape over their mouths, and I bunched and wrapped blankets around each of their heads, ballooning them in size, their forms looking like big matchsticks.

Got Jokes stood by the car, ingesting the plan.

"But I'm the one with the busted hand," Got Jokes said. "So why am I the one loading in the gear?"

"These are complicated times," Trick said.

"Are we breaking up?" he asked her.

"Complicated times," she said again, punching me on the leg so I started to back the Caddy from the lot.

"Where's my Reliant?" Got Jokes said to me.

"Super complicated times," said Trick.

"Where is it, Saint?"

"Like she said," I said, "complicated times!"

"Our drummer," said Trick to Got Jokes (because drummers didn't have names), "will pick you and the gear up. See you at the club."

But Got Jokes was barely listening, pleading with her, "Are these times so complicated that it's *over* over? Maybe this is merely a phase, a blip. There's no way we can work this out?!"

I punched the gas to save him from her answer.

ꝑ

We drove to Sausalito and slid into the near-empty parking lot next to Amy's dying marina. Got Jokes's 1859 Reliant was the only other car when we pulled in, which was good because I'd asked Amy to meet us here. Sure enough, I saw her give us a quick wave from her little boat, before disappearing belowdecks.

Trick and I got out and went to the back of the Caddy. The sun was just starting to set, and we needed to split for Gilman soon, so this was where we'd stash them. On Amy's boat. Out at sea. Their own little Alcatraz.

Because of the fistfight in the Caddy, I'd done something to the tweaker's jaw—broken or dislocated—so when he tried to talk, he sounded like a broken vacuum. Huffs. Sucks. Vowels with their wires shorting out. The big guy was also not doing great, either, spectacularly concussed, bleeding from multiple places on his head, not to mention the crevice the hitter-quitter carved in his thigh. I'd removed the big guy's belt and used it as a tourniquet right above the wound. The bleeding had stopped, and he'd be fine.

Eventually.

Both of them seemed happy that I'd opened the trunk and released them from their vehicular confinement. The sun made them squint, and I remembered that feeling from Quentin, hitting the yard, the sunshine on your face reminding you that you weren't made of papier-mâché.

But both were going to be sorely disappointed when I told them what was about to happen.

"As of right now," I said to them, "you're both collateral. Any questions about that?"

"It sounds like there's a helicopter in my head," the big guy said.

"That's not a question."

He thought for a minute. "Is there a helicopter in my head?"

I turned to Trick. "It's hard to explain things to people crippled with concussions."

"I thought of a better one," the big guy said.

"What?"

"How are we collateral?" he asked, and you could see that he was impressed with himself. "But if I'm being honest, the chopper's my main concern."

"That's your easy problem," Trick said to him.

Then I pointed at the tweaker: "I'm going to trade you for the band's gear."

He issued some vacuum sounds but stopped after a few seconds, in obvious, excruciating pain as his lips vibrated busted consonants.

I pointed at the big guy.

"I probably don't want to know, right?" he said.

"And you're my ticket to meeting with Wes."

I'd taken their phones, checked their contacts, but there was nobody named Wes.

"Is he in your phone under a fake name?"

"Yes. Kenjamin."

Trick and I shot a look at each other: *Did he say Kenjamin?*

"Benjamin?" Trick said, trying to clarify.

"Kenneth?" I said.

"No, Kenjamin."

"That's not a name," said Trick.

"Exactly. It's camouflage," he said.

"It's the opposite of camouflage," she said.

"He's hiding in plain sight in my contacts," the big guy said. "Classic camouflage."

"Benjamin or Ken would be camouflage," Trick said, looking like an aneurysm might be the kind case scenario here. "But since Kenjamin's not a fucking name—"

She was right, of course, but all that mattered was I found Kenjamin's number scrolling through his phone. I interrupted Trick: "He's here."

"The two of you are getting out of the trunk, and you'll behave like fine gentlemen," I said to them, "or I'll beat you to death."

They both nodded. I cut their legs free, and they climbed out, staggered across the planks toward Amy's house. The engine was already fired up on the boat.

I found Amy at the helm, ready to pull out to sea.

I was the warden of my own little Alcatraz.

Too bad Denis couldn't see me now.

# 10

MY FATHER SAID, "After six years of you training, you're ready to learn to hunt with a bow, boy, like our forefathers. It is now forbidden. Can you imagine, outlawing somebody's history—our lineage? The modern Norwegian government says we aren't allowed to hunt with a bow, but just because these bureaucrat Christians are willing to piss on our history, we won't, boy. We will keep our ancestors alive. We'll hunt through the cold and the quiet. We'll eat organs. Roast flesh over an open flame."

We started on the hay bale in his yard, learning to draw, to nock, breathe, release. We wore our bows on our backs during our animal crawls. "You move on four legs like this, and you'll have a back knotted in muscle, strong as an oarsman's."

We started with stationary targets. Dummies he'd plant in the forest. Then we moved to brown rats, a scrawny trophy for a scrawny boy.

Now, if you've never attempted to hit a rodent with a bow and arrow, let me say it presented its challenges.

Namely, those rats were fast, and my skills were still remedial.

It was only desperation, animal desperation, that finally helped me kill one.

It was my father saying he wouldn't give me anything else to eat.

Until I killed a rat.

I went out into the woods with my bow early in the morning and came home famished as the sun set, and he asked, "Well?" and I said, "Nothing, Tron," and he said, "You're hungry?" and I said, "I am," and he said, "Aim better in the morning."

Which I did not.

No breakfast.

Because of all the hiking, I was getting lightheaded by lunch.

By the late afternoon, I was dizzy, seeing double.

Sundown, I returned home, and it shamed me how badly I wanted to cry, and it shamed me that I wanted to beg him for food. I had failed, and because of that, I was starving. He wanted me to learn the old ways and I couldn't do anything right.

Rats.

I was being outsmarted by rats.

My father handed me a mug of bone broth. "Drink. Sit by the fire."

My hands shook violently as I brought it to my chapped face. I finished the mug in a sip, burped, drooled, handed it back to him. Then I crashed in front of the fire. My father went and ladled more bone broth into my mug, sat next to me in front of the fire, rubbing my leg.

"More?" he said.

"I'm sorry."

"For what?"

"I can't do it."

He nudged me with the mug until I took it, drank from it, a warmth slithering through me for the first time in two days.

"Tomorrow, should we go out together?" he said.

"Yes, Tron. Thank you."

"If it makes you feel any better," he said, "I haven't eaten in two days, too."

"That makes me feel worse."

"If a man doesn't lead by example, he's weak," he said. "And we are never going to be weak, boy."

I hoisted my broth at him. "Here, please, sorry."

"Stop apologizing. This is solidarity."

"Solidarity that I can't kill rats?"

"Because I'm teaching you—because we are a pack." He pushed the mug back toward me. "That's for you."

I finished it, again, in a ravenous sip, my chin slick with fat and grease. We watched the fire crackle while our hungry guts did the same.

I wiped the fat and grease off my chin and licked it from my fingers.

"I'm sorry we're hungry," I said.

"Tomorrow, we eat."

"Do we eat the rats we kill?"

"What do you think we do in Norway, ski and eat rat stew?"

"I'm so hungry I'd eat rat stew," I said.

"You know what? So would I. Good thing our family passes down a rat stew recipe. I'll teach it to you next."

We both cracked up. It was the time with him that I remember laughing the hardest.

It was the hunger; it was the love.

I swear to you that sitting by that fire with bone broth sloshing in my stomach, on the borderline of a hunger hallucination, laughing with my father about rat stew, might be the happiest memory of my life.

My father stood, retrieved the mug. His eyes were glossed with laughter, and he said, "Here, let me get you some more."

Þ

Amy cut the engine a couple hundred feet from shore. The ocean was calm, and the sun was quickly going down.

She agreed to stand guard over them. Jesse was on board, too, crashed out on the bathroom floor. He'd wanted to take another bath, but he needed to get sick again and fell asleep on the floor in front of the toilet instead.

Now, I was looking down on these matchstick men I'd made.

Their duct-taped straight bodies.

Their heads wrapped in blankets.

They were on the floor of Amy's living room, and because the blankets were black, they looked like huge matches, waiting for a giant to light them up.

I crouched down, lowered my head over them to amplify my voice, to make sure they could hear me beneath those layers of blankets.

"Men," I said, "this wasn't the day any of us thought we'd be having over our Pop-Tarts this morning. I was changing the strings on my Tele when fate called me on this quest. But now we move to a new phase. You will sit, wrapped up like this, for hours. It will be uncomfortable, and you deserve it. You are on a ship in the bay, and with your injuries, swimming for shore is impossible. I'm also leaving you under the watch of an armed guard, who will shoot you in the stomach if you decide not to stay still like good little matchsticks."

Amy threw her hands up at me: *I don't have a gun.*

And I shrugged: *Don't sweat it, I'm only scarin' 'em.*

Then I said to the matchsticks, "I'll be back in a few hours. We'll all go see Wes and end all this. Sound good? It should. This is the only way you survive."

I stopped talking to gauge if either of the matchsticks attempted a verbal response behind the thick tapestries. I had been too close when that shotgun went off and didn't know if my hearing was impaired.

I waited five seconds to be polite.

Not a mumble from the matchsticks.

"Man," Trick said, standing next to me. I'd forgotten that she was there. She gave me serious side-eye. "You are dark, Saint."

I stood back up, whispered to her so their head blankets would block my words. "It's hyperbole."

"I don't know what that word means," said Trick.

"Neither did I. Learned about it in a writing class. It's when you exaggerate for effect."

"Hyperbole."

"Yeah."

"It must have been an incredible class, because you're nailing it."

"I took it in prison. You should probably know that about me."

"I'm fine with you doing time," she said, "but I wish you didn't use words like *hyperbole*."

ᚦ

Amy prepped the dinghy that Trick and I would row back to shore. Then I would drive the Caddy to the concert. But before that could happen, I needed to call Wes.

It was time.

I stood alone on the deck, watching the waves around the boat. It was choppier out here, and the wind was much more potent than on shore. There were no other vessels close to us, though there was a tanker coming under the Golden Gate, a few sailboats passing in front of the sun as it touched the horizon.

I dialed his number.

One time, on an animal crawl, my belly close to the earth, as I moved on all fours, on my paws, I'd stumbled across a praying mantis eating a wasp. The mantis had a sturdy grip on its prey, and the wasp was still alive and its wings beat as fast as they could, the stinger attempting to reach the mantis, but it was no use, as the mantis had such a size advantage and its body was positioned in front of the wasp, which meant the mantis was going to eat it in two ways: It was going to eat it while the wasp was still alive, and the praying mantis was going to eat the head first.

The head!

What a death to have your face eaten before you made it to Valhalla at the hands of your enemy.

After nibbling the head, the mantis ate the flapping wings.

After the wings, the wasp was folded in half, so the mantis could suck the innards. All the while the wasp's legs pedaled in midair.

Still alive, helpless to defend itself.

And that was what I was going to do to him.

Wes the wasp.

On the third ring, he answered. "Yes, this is a man called Kenjamin. Capricorn, ninja, truant officer," he said.

I knew he was a real person, of course, but as soon as I heard his voice, I understood what the big guy had meant: I could feel a helicopter's rotors spinning in me, my brain chugging in circles, threatening to tear off my skull.

"My name is Saint, and your friends are having a bad fucking day," I said.

He didn't skip a beat: "Kenjamin is a family name. Passed down by priests and mechanics and mercenaries. My mother was so short you could see her feet in her driver's license photo."

"We need to meet," I said. "Tonight."

"Ooh, sorry, I've got a previous engagement at the International Space Station to witness the separation of conjoined twins. They only have one soul, so it's going to be tricky."

I had to wonder if, in his mayhem mind, he could really understand the danger here. Wes wasn't tracking that I'd do anything, didn't get that I'd bruise everybody to protect musicians. The people, mostly blue collar, who scraped together their savings to buy pawn shop instruments and amps and drums and mics. We'd sell whatever we had to so that we could make our noise. We had something to say, and we didn't care that no one wanted to hear our songs. That was why our art was pure; that was what made it passion. And because I held our punk rock in such esteem, I wouldn't let anyone corrupt our melodies of escape.

"Hear me," I said to Wes, "this is your only chance to get your men back."

"Let me see if I can clear my calendar. RoboCop. Hoboken. Hey, Alexa, play Dysentery."

"If I don't hear from you by midnight—"

"You're a diamond in the buff," he said, "a real schizophrenic juggernaut, an aardvark on an acid trip. Laffy Taffy."

"If I don't hear from you by midnight, they're going in the bay, all tied up."

"Oh, you and I will talk, and we will see each other soon," he said. "I hate to see you go, Saint, but I love to watch you bleed."

And he hung up.

It was time.

The Vikings in my blood went mum. I couldn't hear anything except Tron's dead voice: *Be the book.*

I poked my head inside the houseboat and told Trick I'd meet her onshore, which was met with a puzzled mug, her *huh* face . . .

And I turned right around and ran to the edge of the deck, and I dove into the water, the cold. There was low visibility when I tried to stare down into the frigid murk. Gazing, maybe, fifteen feet in the darkness.

But I didn't need to see much. I knew exactly where I was going.

My body was shocked and alert and alive.

I dove into the possibilities of this night.

I could sense every fish and mammal within a hundred miles.

I knew all the trash tangled in the seaweed.

I talked to the ocean, and it couldn't believe all the garbage, all the secrets we dumped into it so that we kept our consciences cleaned, wiping them off like baby birds after a tanker spill.

I knew these great white sharks circling the Farallon Islands, hungry for hunt and blubber. They hadn't evolved in millions of years because they were perfect at their calling. I'd never heard anyone ask if sharks were smart, and yet, they must be. That balance between the brains in your head and the teeth in your mouth. That devouring purpose.

Yes, the wonder of swimming freestyle as fast as I could toward shore . . .

Yes, the elation of my limbs carrying me closer to the Caddy, the concert . . .

Toward Wes . . .

I opened my eye, and the salt water burned, and it was beautiful.

Do you understand that?

A fucking drug.

A fucking drug called joy.

ᚠ

"Do you hear my glass birds?" my father said, waking me in the morning.

My stomach growled so loudly it sounded like it had a distortion pedal. When I wasn't starving to death, I played the electric guitar eight hours a day. When I wasn't starving to death, I dreamed of Iggy and happy monsters.

"Your birds?" I asked.

"You can't hear them?"

"I don't think so."

"They are going to help us hunt these rats," he said.

"I don't understand."

"Be happy," he said. "They'll make sure we eat today." He stopped talking and looked to the ceiling, the sky—he saw something up there that no one else could, and his jaw went slack, his eyes surprised, staring. Finally, to me: "You really don't hear that?"

"No."

"It's like the whole sky is an orchestra pit," he said. "I hear them all."

"I can't hear anything."

"You will, boy. Before it's all said and done, you'll have your own birds." He pulled the blanket off me. "Let's go."

And we were out of the house fast, after another dose of bone broth for fuel, we were in our animal crawls, bows on our backs. We snuck slowly watching the ground, making our way down toward the river. It was a cold morning, but this was Norway. Your coat got thick.

"All the boys of Norway won't know the bow. These bureaucrats. These leeches. Sucking the blood of our history. Our traditions."

"Can I ask you about the boys of Norway?" I said.

"What is it?"

"You told me of boys whose fathers changed their given names to something from the Old World, but you never did that for me."

"I thought you liked being James."

"I do."

"But you want a Viking name."

"Yes."

Tron stopped walking, put his hand on my chest so I couldn't go on. "It would be my honor to give you a Viking name," he said.

"Yes."

"It has to be formidable."

"Yes."

"It needs to be brutal."

"Yes."

"Your new name is Fenrir," he said.

"What does it mean?"

"Son of Loki and Angerboda. Fenrir is a monstrous wolf."

"Fenrir is a monstrous wolf," I said, smiling.

We heard it at the same time. A rustle at the base of a stump, fifteen feet off. We aimed the bows. He nodded at me. I shot first.

And I got it.

My father started prowling around like a wolf, howling at the bright morning sky. "And you," he said, "let me hear you howl."

I pulled in as much air as possible, lungs stretching, hurting—and then letting it explode out in an animal call, head shaking back and forth, feral.

"You did it," he said.

"Let's keep going. I want to shoot more."

"Okay, I'll follow you."

He was teaching me the way of our elders, and I had made my first kill with the bow and I had wrestled a bear and the Old World was flowing through me, through us, my years with Tron had settled into a kind of aggressive happiness. It was tough and fast, but we cared about each other, more every day, every hunt—and he said, "I'll follow you," and that meant that he was behind me, watching my back, watching out for me, naming me, finally, I had people, finally, my people, my person, finally.

Fenrir was a monstrous wolf.

Out of the corner of my eye I saw a rat by a rock pile. I took a shot and hit it. My father saw one poke its head out of a log, and Tron took the shot, missing high, the arrow heading down to the river.

"Damn," he said, "I'm rusty."

"Don't worry. I'll get enough for both of us."

"That's very nice of you."

"I agree."

"How about I go make us a stack of pancakes?" he said. "But sadly, no rats."

"The pancakes will have to do."

"We need to go get that arrow," he said. "You never leave something like that in nature."

We continued our animal crawl, and soon we came to the clearing by the river. That was when we saw him: a fisherman.

A fisherman lying on the shore.

A fisherman lying on the shore with the arrow sticking out of his face.

A fisherman lying on the shore with the arrow sticking out of his face, and he was dead.

I didn't know what to do and looked to my father for guidance, but he was again staring straight up, transfixed by something. I had no idea what he saw or heard, but I did know one thing: Whatever it was, it was beautiful. And that made this moment so strange to witness, a man looking with awe toward the heavens, while a dead man lay close by with an arrow jutting from his face.

"That was," said my father, "not supposed to happen."

"Is he dead?" I asked.

"He is the most dead you can be." He looked up toward the sky again and said to it, "Don't you think I know that?" Then he spoke to me: "We have a problem, boy. A big one. And because of that, I'd like to tell you a story. Is that okay with you?"

"Yes, Father."

"Tron."

"Yes, Tron."

"I like having you live with me."

"Me, too."

"These six years have been . . . unplanned magic."

"Unplanned magic?"

"Okay, here's the story: I once drank a potion made of henbane, and it let me see my death. I know how I'm supposed to die, boy. It may seem like the kind of thing that would be corrosive to learn, but I found it freeing. I knew how much time I had. I knew how much life I'd been given and could prioritize accordingly. So because I know this, my prized secret, I want you to hear it, too. So you can possess this story, because it's a pleasant way to go. I got lucky. There are some real grim ways to go, but I got this. Picture a ship, big, sleek. There is a barbecue happening on the sundeck. A group of friends eating lobsters in bathing suits. There's a jazz band playing, a mournful singer with a marvelous, big ass, and she makes the whole room want to screw. We are drinking champagne. People keep coming up and congratulating me. Apparently, in this future, I win a prestigious award. I just make the glass birds because it's the only way to shut them up, boy—you know this—but this party is to celebrate my accomplishments. Never care about accolades, they are venom, they are"—he pointed to the dead man—"arrows to your face. Those traps will kill you if you ever need their praise to create. That's not how real artists work. No, our fuel is self-sustaining. Let the whores have fame. We have the work. And I could do the birds because I knew I'd live to seventy-three, the day on the yacht, when everyone is in bathing suits listening to jazz, and we dance and eat lobsters, and it was so decadent and dumb and so unlike me to be in a posh setting, but I let it all go that day, that day in the future after I won the award, that day I die. I take a break from dancing, sit down at a table overlooking the ocean. There is nothing to see except water and sky, and as I stare, I suddenly get tired, so tired that I'd like to lie down for a minute—no, that will take too long to get to a bed, instead I'll just rest my head here on this table, yes, that's better, that feels right, my head feels drunk and ready, and it's all getting slow and dark and . . . well, that's it, boy. That's how I die."

"That sounds nice," I said.

"It was a false future, I guess. That's one thing you can say about these lives of ours: The last surprise is the biggest one of all."

"What are we going to do about him?" I asked my father, pointing to the dead man.

But my father gazed to the sky again, listening, nodding, saying, "I know. Don't you think I know that?" Then he said to me, "You're a good boy. Iggy Pop would have been lucky to have you as a son."

Then my father pulled out his knife, gripped it in front of his chest. His breathing changed, big breaths, in and out.

"Tron!"

He didn't answer me.

Big breaths.

"Tron!"

He didn't answer me.

Big breaths.

"Tron!"

My father said, "Your mother has a sister in San Francisco. They haven't spoken in years. Get to her."

"Dad!"

"A pagan can't survive in a cage," he said.

"Please, Dad, please!"

"We need the open air to fill our sails," he said, and we locked eyes.

A father.

A son.

A pack.

The best years of my life.

Then Tron slit his throat.

There were two dead men now.

I fell to my knees.

There was nobody who knew I was Fenrir.

The three of us, by the river.

# 11

TRICK PARKED a couple blocks away, off San Pablo Avenue, and we marched toward 924 Gilman Street. The sun was down now. At this time of night, this stretch of Berkeley blossomed with anarchy.

People living in their street tents rose from the dead and zipped them open, crawling from their synthetic crypts to score. And the ones who didn't get high but were wasted on memories and mental illnesses—they, too, roamed the sidewalks and made small talk with their traumas, wondering what the weather looked like without childhood flashbacks.

And no boomtown would be complete without illegal commerce, hustlers hocking stolen goods, sex (its own kind of stolen good), and all manner of drugs that turned your brain into a TV show directed by Salvador Dalí.

Because we were so close to the ocean, there was usually a briny reek, but tonight, the neighborhood had a different smell: Somebody grilled bacon-wrapped hot dogs out of their minivan's slide door, pumping mariachi music, and this was a bacon world, thank you very much, and if you found yourself here, it came with a complimentary perfume of cured pig.

"Should we get a hot dog?" I said, as we navigated the maze of tents and shrapnel.

"Should we eat something that will make us shit ourselves onstage?" she said. "Yeah, let's not."

Trick had been quiet since leaving the matchsticks on Amy's houseboat, and I needed to check in, make sure she was getting ready to rock tonight. "How do you feel?" I asked her.

"A little tired after rowing that fucking dinghy."

"I'm sorry," I said, "but I had to feel the water."

"Yeah, and I had to fucking row that dinghy," she said.

I hoped that saying this next thing would immediately cheer her up, the way that thinking about it made me happy. "And now we get to make music," I said.

"To a packed house."

"That's what I was trying to ask before. How do you feel about the show?"

"I don't get nervous, if that's what you're asking,"

"I'm asking how you're feeling."

"I wish we'd practiced more, but it was . . . a full day."

"We're ready," I said. "The songs sound dialed."

"I know, that's what scares me," she said. "You picked them up so fast; either you can shred or our songs suck."

"Simple is best. Ask Bad Brains."

We were approaching a busker, who played an acoustic guitar like it used to hit the man's mother. He had a cardboard sign in front of him that said HI, MY NAME IS ELON BUSK.

"Do you think they'll like my songs?" Trick asked.

"I think you're about to tear the roof off that place," I said.

She stopped walking. I stopped, too. Mr. Busk was still curb-stomping that guitar and playing to an audience of ghosts. Trick had a serious expression on her face—focused, yes, but I could also see calculus zoom through her eyes. She was scrolling through her options.

And while all that math was going on inside Trick, here was what was happening in me as I watched her: I was developing the instinct to track down anything that ever caused her pain and beat it to death, an instinct called love.

Then I thought something so gross, so appalling, that I don't even want to tell you, but no need to censor all my barking in your brain, that supernatural silo, that foreclosed moral code. Here was the truly disgusting thought I had: If I ever wrote a song for Trick, it would be called "I'd Fight Lightning for You."

Then, as though she could read my mind, she said, "I like your songs, and do you like mine?"

"I could play these songs with you every day and do nothing else with my life and die satisfied."

She squinted up at me. "Stop being so intense."

"I don't know how."

"And promise me you won't puke on yourself onstage," she said. "This really matters to me, okay? Don't fuck it up."

"I won't."

"You can't."

"Hey, speaking of being onstage," I said. "I bought something at the army supply store. Something I'd like to wear onstage."

"What is it?"

I leaned and whispered in her ear. I hoped she liked the idea.

But it's not time for you to know, not yet.

Then she smiled at me, hit me on the arm, asking, "Is there any left for me?"

ᚡ

We rounded the corner, both looked up to the cross streets.

The corner of Eighth and Gilman. The cross streets of our punk rock paradise.

There was already a line of punks down the block, frothing to hear Jawbreaker. Security out patrolling the street in red t-shirts, trying to make a bunch of crusties stand in line, was like dealing with a bunch of Weimaraners on speed. An impossible ask. Too many teenagers. Too many people on drugs. Too many tempers. Too many childhoods that rolled from the assembly line defective. Too many minds that housed neurodivergent angels. Too much testosterone. Too much malt liquor.

The entrance to 924 Gilman Street was brick, tagged, and stickered up.

There it was, right in front of us, our pagan temple.

We stood still for a minute. Trick held my hand. Then we approached. A woman with a clipboard, huge feathered earrings, Celtic patterns running in sleeves down her arms. Her hair striped gray and burgundy. "All the Fuss! Wilma!" she said, kissing Trick on the mouth. She pointed to me. "This must be the guy who broke Got Jokes's hand."

"You heard about that, huh?" I said.

"He's telling everyone." Then she leaned in closer to us. "The consensus is you did the right thing." She turned her attention back to Trick. "I can't wait to hear you tonight. Come on, let's go inside," and we followed her, past security, the ticket counter.

Gilman was a haven for us strays, but it told you who it was and what mattered in this club, its rules splattered on the wall:

**NO ALCOHOL NO DRUGS NO VIOLENCE NO STAGE DIVING NO DOGS NO FUCKED UP BEHAVIOR NO RACISM NO MISOGYNY/SEXISM NO HOMOPHOBIA NO TRANSPHOBIA.**

Yes, a lot of punks fudged on the booze and drugs part, but so long as you could abide by most of those few rules, Gilman wanted you to feel the fire of tonight's show.

You're a person and I'm a person, and since we're standing in this holy site together, let's look around the main room, up to the stage, and please allow me to wallop you with a flurry of the ol' broken baroque, exuberantly bending language with my brand of bad taste, as we take in this godhouse, this pulverizing megaphone, this insecure sensei, this allergy attack, this electric chair, this street poet, this hatchery, this pet store, this greasy spoon, a gold tooth, a sweet tooth, a sour lover, a leather jacket, a funeral home, a foster home, a looted schizophrenia, an amplifier, a longship, an infected piercing, a combat boot, a dumpster dive, a leaky waterbed, a king, a queen, a record collection, a parent, a jester, a spaceship, a caseworker, a panhandler, a bully, a parachute, a fireworks show.

Gilman's walls seemed to have multiple personality disorder, a constant onslaught of art and graffiti, stickers and tags. You'd find logos stenciled and flyers wheat-pasted to walls. Before something even had the time to dry, another punk was claiming that bit of space for their own, the whole room was a body that was always getting its tattoos covered up, and covered up, and covered up . . .

The heart here ran on one thing: throwing wild shows. Things so loud and raucous, so out of tune at 924, that the world was a speeding ambulance ride, and you were in the back getting thrown around, your gurney slamming into walls, but whatever was wrong with you, suddenly you were cured, you stood tall in the back of the ambulance, and the music hit like adrenaline, that dirty electricity.

Gilman gave us exactly what we wanted. Shows for everybody. Unknown bands, some national, some locals who hit huge—and by that I meant huge to the circle of people who mattered to us. Screw 32. Crimpshrine. Neurosis. Spitboy. Swingin' Utters. The Mr. T Experience. Tilt. Melvins. NOFX. One Man Army. American Steel. The godfathers, Op Ivy, and some of their members went on to form Rancid, who could've sold out, but those boys kept it pure, staying indie on Epitaph Records. They never left the cult of what we worshipped: integrity.

There were people who thought integrity was a deadweight, but lugging our integrity around was what made punks so strong. The people at Gilman were loyal until we weren't. Ask Jello from the DKs, who was punk rock royalty back in the day—but in '94 Jello got stomped, the pit going to work on him, kicking him, breaking his leg, hollering in his face, "Rich rock star, rich rock star."

By loyalty, I meant to the scene. The music was a meritocracy. If you could play, take the stage. That was all that mattered. If you had it, we wanted to hear it.

And Trick Wilma was the real deal, and tonight, I'd be standing next to her.

ᛈ

I repasted my mohawk in liberty spikes, and I drenched each in the reflective paint I'd bought at Hild's. Yes, now is time for you to know—and see me crowned in radioactive antlers. Trick Wilma, too, used the reflective paint on her eyebrows, like neon lipstick, put streaks in her hair.

We walked onstage, and the punks looked at me like I'd gazed at those reindeers with lightning bolts growing from their heads.

As our set started, Trick pounded out the opening riff of the first song on her bass, low and slow, and then I let the guitar flower with feedback. The drummer banged her toms, the kick drum thumping quick quarter notes, and now I let my happy monster do its thing, getting gritty, sleazy, the song crunchy, fast—and the room threw a few sparks at the song, warming to us. The heads started nodding and the shoulders started swinging, and these punks all went up in flames, the whole room combusted, wild with fire.

And the rush of watching the swarm move, putting a pit together, circling, slamming, camaraderie in friendly battle. And it wasn't just seeing their madness as they stomped, no, it was that our song incited their energy, our song demanded their bodies crash. The room turned into one rank armpit, I could taste our briny sweat, I could see our song slide in their ears and turn these punks into derby cars—and it came over me onstage, a comfort, I was watching a riot break out before my eye, and this was my home, I wanted to live here, this was the high I'd always been chasing, I had to find a way to do this every night of my life.

It wasn't just wunjo anymore—now it was something better.

Purpose.

Being onstage with Trick was a celestial event.

In what felt like nine seconds, the song ended, and they howled at us.

We were in.

Trick smiled at me, and she said to the crowd, "This is our new guitarist, Saint. He joined the band this afternoon. He rewrote most of the guitar parts today, the maniac. Everyone say 'Hi, Saint!'"

"Hi, Saint!" they said.

Got Jokes put his head in his hands.

"Anything you'd like to tell these crusties, Saint?" Trick Wilma asked me in the mic.

Never dawned on me that crowd work was on the menu. I was already trying to remember new guitar parts to new songs, and now—what—I was supposed to charm?

I had nothing.

They gave me a two-second grace period, which for punks was unexpected and generous in duration. Then they came with the wisecracks, the catcalls, revving to heckle.

I tried to say something true to them, something so they'd know who I really was, something Viking. So I yelled into the mic with my warrior face on: "I don't care if I live or die, and that's what's both great and terrifying about me."

What followed was the quietest beat I ever heard in a punk club.

Then a voice from the back of the crowd: "Welcome, Saint the Terrifying!" And then they all started screaming at us to get back to work. To play.

Trick counted us in, and we were off sprinting into her next song. We played the next half hour, sloppy and fast and reckless, and they didn't care about any mistakes we made in our execution. How could they? This wasn't a recital. This was punk rock.

It was Trick's screeching melodies, her aggression.

Our songs possessed the energy of a Viking with a sword in one hand and an ax in the other.

Our songs didn't care if they lived or died, and that was both great and terrifying about them.

þ

Our set ended, and I bowed, let my guitar intentionally fall victim to gravity, the strap coming up my back, my neck, my head, and the guitar crashing to the floor, feedback wailing, and I leaped into the crowd, landing on my feet, standing tall among my brothers and sisters.

"Saint the Terrifying," they said, and we laughed together. A few reached out to touch my radioactive antlers, and I let them.

I was in a new country. Not that I hadn't been in this land before. I spent many a night in Gilman, and I was known and liked okay. Never, though, did people interact with me in this capacity. Never, though, did I interact with them like this, because before now, I'd never known my purpose. The crowd, like me, heard Trick's whole record performed tonight, and we knew this truth: She was a star. All the Fuss needed to cut that record on the quick.

I moved among them, and we were a filthy civilization, and the whole moment couldn't possibly be any better.

I was living the life that Tron wanted for me.

I was being the book.

I was Fenrir the monstrous wolf.

And I wanted to stay with them so badly. It was all that I wanted to do.

Some punks kept calling, "Saint the Terrifying, Saint the Terrifying," and they touched my radioactive antlers.

Instead of staying with them, though, I fought toward the door. I moved away from Trick, from our show, from the music, the pack. It was the last thing I wanted to do, but it was required of me.

I moved into the darkness, alone, toward Wes Than Zero.

ᚦ

Here was a tall tale—one that began with betrayal, as these kinds of stories kicked off. It launched with a man who wore a mustache but called it a dustache, a man whom I would've called a fast friend yesterday, but no longer, no need, no use—because this man revealed himself to be greedy.

Now before continuing, you need to know that I, the teller of this tall tale, despised the epidemic called "capitalism" that turned people into greed weasels. Into agents of Wanting More. Into joyless collectors of junk. Into desperate nymphomaniacs, spread-eagled and fucking themselves with their Amazon Prime accounts.

Greed weasels.

That was how I saw the average citizen. That was who I knew they were, even while they acquired a new target, a new conquest, a new kill . . .

Okay, so now that you understand the hatred I had for the greed weasels, let's get back to the man who wore the dustache, a former ally but now a turncoat, yes, this was the second that Dusty ambushed me in the parking lot at Amy's marina.

I'd been drunk on Feeling the whole ride over from Gilman, extravagantly high from being onstage with Trick. So that made me buzz with joy, and I was also the warden returning to his tiny Alcatraz, which added more distortion, more volume, more noise in me.

I called Amy on the ride over and asked her to bring the boat in. Told her I'd be there soon. And I was. Got out of the ride, and that was when Dusty's cab screeched into the parking lot. He parked a couple spaces down from me and hopped out, leaned on his hood.

Just a greed weasel with his dustache, calm as can be.

I didn't like that he leaned on the hood of his car, our place of employment. I know this sounded super Whole Foods, but it was where we logged long hours, where we were friends. But now we were here, and now we were not friends.

There were three men sitting in Dusty's car, sitting in the place that used to be mine. Just fucking sitting there.

"Nice hair," Dusty said to me, pointing at my radioactive antlers.

"What do you want?"

"I'm here offering you a last chance."

Last chance? Couldn't he see that I was surrounded by glass birds?

"Last chance. That's interesting," I said. "What's weird is the last time I saw you, you said you just needed to go *talk* to Wes—and now here we are here, at my last chance. Sounds like a lot has changed."

"I don't know that it needs to sound that way."

"Which way?"

"What if nobody makes any choices?"

"That's the thing about us," I said. "We are always making choices."

"Do you know what I first said to him when he asked what you were like?" Dusty said.

"What?"

"I said, 'Wes, he knocks out monsters.'"

"That's actually funny, Dust, because earlier, I went swimming and thought about sharks. They're a kind of monster. And I was wondering what was more important: the brains in our heads or the teeth in our mouths."

"Which one is it?" Dusty said.

My fingers, for whatever reason, flew together for fists. "I'm about to show you."

Dusty pointed to his pals in the car. "Don't forget about them."

"I won't."

"Brains or teeth," he said. "Which one do you think it is?"

Maybe there was no way for me to explain it to him. I barely understood it myself. But I couldn't shake the idea that there were just too many hearts in this world, competing for the last splats of food. We were all starving, could feel it squeal in our guts. This call to find joy. And that could haunt you and gnarl you and kick you and make you mean—or that call could make you live sick with recklessness, like me, which meant you could howl at the fucking moon and watch your music make it cry.

But Dusty couldn't wait to quench his heart, couldn't wait to do it right. So he cut the line.

And that was how we ended up in a deserted parking lot, save for his three new friends in the cab, what used to be our cab.

"Now I see that it's not just the teeth and the head," I said to Dusty. "It's also your heart."

"Whose heart?" Dusty asked.

"Yours," I said.

"I saw the first half of your set tonight," he said, still leaning casually on the hood. "I had to leave for obvious reasons. So we could wait for you outside and follow. So you could bring us here."

"What did you think of the show?" I asked.

"It's hard to admit this, but you already sound better with them than our crap band."

"About that," I said, "I quit Slummy."

"I figured."

Now it was my turn to point to his three new friends in the car. "I don't think they'll get out," I said, "once they see what I do to you."

"What are you about to do to me?"

"I don't think they have the balls."

"Do I have to guess?"

"Just tell me why, Dust," I said. "We were fucking tight."

"If it was up to me, we'd still be tight after this. If it was up to me, you'd fucking understand that working for Wes is my only way to make real money. I work for him five more years, I can retire to Costa Rica. It's the only way I can get ahead. If I live poor down there, I can be free. Why can't you just let it go? Who cares what Wes is doing? It doesn't matter."

"So you're choosing money."

"I don't want to choose anything," said Dusty. "We don't have to choose. That's what I'm trying to say to you."

"I'm watching you get mind-fucked by your own cop-out. It's fascinating."

"This is the only way a guy like me gets to Costa Rica."

"I like Oakland just fine," I said, and it was time.

Have you ever bitten off somebody's finger? Neither had I.

I shot toward Dusty and snatched him from his car's hood. I hit him in the solar plexus so he couldn't breathe, so he was a short-term scarecrow, hollow of any capacity to defend himself. I had a mouth, oh yes, I had a mouth that had an immense appetite to chew, to give a gnash on a digit, yes, before I knew it, one of his fingers had slipped into my mouth and first it was meat, then bone, and with a few sharklike shakes of my head I had the whole finger lopped off and in my mouth, the blood dripping to my chin, beading into a drop, raining from me, an almost beautiful feeling until, realizing it was from my friend's finger, I threw Dusty over my shoulder, and I spun the two of us in a tight circle, gaining kinetic energy, whirling us as fast as I could, Dusty's limbs looking like a floppy propeller, and then I launched him at the windshield of his car, crashing, the glass spiderwebbing immediately and startling the new friends, who sat ogling the action, dumbstruck and entertained, as I took Dusty's finger out of my mouth, and I went to the driver's-side window and used the blood from the finger's wound as a red Magic

Marker and drew a smeary question mark on the window, and I shouted at these new friends, "How many fucking fingers would you like to leave here with?" and one of them crawled behind the steering wheel, turned the key, started the engine, hit the gas, this clown car full of tough punks speeding out of the parking lot.

# WHOLE FOODS HALLUCINATION

'M, SOMEHOW, here again.

Billie is, somehow, working.

Even rock stars have to keep the lights on. Fucking gig economy.

We're at his register, and he's ringing up my box of thirty-dollar artisan Pop-Tarts.

The small talk is music related. We're doing what musicians do: talk shit. We're talking about how some bands are so awful that merely mentioning their names can make you laugh.

Here.

Let's try.

Third Eye Blind.

Then this old shriveled white guy comes up behind me and plops his basket on the conveyor belt, too hard, and Billie and I both go quiet and turn to look. The old man has that Gollum angel-hair head. Linty scalp. He is wearing a secondhand suit.

He says to us, "Gentlemen, let's address the elephant in the room right now: Yes, you are in fact talking to 'Boogie in Your Butt' royalty.

That's how I do it. Straight to the point. Yes, that 1982 classic song by one Eddie Murphy—sweet Jesus, that man could sing—and we collaborated on it together, the two of us."

Billie's conveyor belt is just running and running—he's stunned—and the man's basket hits Billie's hand, and he doesn't even notice. He can't take his eyes off this old man.

I dig him, too. He talks like Weird Al doing a eulogy.

And so the man keeps going: "Yes, we made it all the way to lucky number fifty-seven on the R&B charts. We did that. There are a lot—I'm talking a stadium full of world-class musicians—who never made it to fifty-fucking-seven on the charts. Eddie and me, we climbed that Everest together."

"I'm calling bullshit," says Billie, pulling his phone out of his Whole Foods apron. "What's your name? I'm looking you up."

"I go by Bud Carruthers."

Billie paws at his phone, then smirks and nods, then says to Bud, "Yeah, well, the internet says that Eddie Murphy cowrote that track with a dude named David Wolfert," and Bud Carruthers starts huffing hearing that name, and Bud Carruthers says, "Oh, sure, they wrote the song—but I inspired the song because I lived the song, and I gifted it to Eddie. I wanted him to have it."

"So you didn't write the song, or you did?" I ask.

"How do you live a song that someone else wrote, man?" Billie asks.

"Every song ever written requires inspiration," says Bud Carruthers. "Without that, no song. No song, no 'Boogie in Your Butt.'"

"And you inspired it how?"

"I met Eddie Murphy, only once, at a party. My cousin is big on Broadway, and they had mutual friends. So one night our paths crossed. I was not my best self in this era. I was making what we'll call 'bad decisions.' And I needed money. It was late at the party. I'd already been asked to leave. And hey, I was high. Like I said, bad decisions, and I jokingly asked someone if they'd give me a dollar if I shoved my thumb in my ass before I left, and they said they would, and so I did the act, and so they paid me, and I washed my thumb and had twenty bucks, and the room's attitude toward me turned in my favor—suddenly, I was unasked to leave, I was reinvited to the party for some reason, and I was really high—bad decisions—and my antics intrigued that degenerate gene in the other party guests, I guess, because then they started asking me if I'd stick certain other things in my butt for sums of money, and I said of course—what, do you think I'm an idiot?—and their requests started off reasonably, small stakes, like I said, reasonably—that's how it started. There was a small, collectible rock; there was a small, travel-sized clock; there was a small, novelty tin can; there was a miniature model of a man—these items went in my butt, and Eddie was in the room—and that's just the first verse of the song. I inserted other props that grew in mass and stature, just like in the song, but since some of them awaken haunted memories in me, I'd like to avoid discussing them—these being the unreasonably sized items I alluded to earlier, so we can skip over them—let's get to the best example. Later in the song, Eddie clearly sings, 'Put a clown in your butt,' and at that party, on the night in question, for fifty dollars, I put a figurine of a clown in my butt, and I know that Eddie witnessed the act because of his signature laugh, a laugh that's so unique it could only be him. I heard that laugh, and that laugh was his inspiration—my butt, a muse—and that's the night I wrote a hit fucking song with Eddie Murphy."

"What's the point of that story?" Billie asks.

"The point of the story is," the old man says, "that was my fifteen minutes of fame. And you guys are lucky. Billie, your fifteen is lasting forever, and Saint, we don't know about you yet. You might get a fifteen minutes that's been kissed by an angel, like Billie did—but you might get one like me, fifteen minutes of ass fame. I'm saying mine already happened, and I'm saying yours is coming, Saint. Do something with it."

And in that moment, I feel the urge to weep. I don't, of course. I won't. But it's right there, like there's personality to these tears. Like I'm excited to see a friend.

"How much money did you make that night?" I ask Bud.

"Eight hundred dollars."

"Not a bad take."

"A man suffers for his art," the old man says, and he pats down a few stray hairs on his mostly exposed scalp.

Then we all hear it, right at the same time. We blossom with recognition when we hear his laugh, Eddie Murphy's signature one, coming from the produce section.

"I should go say hi," the old man says.

"Follow your gut," Billie says.

"How do I look?" the man asks us.

My first instinct here is to be cruel to him, and I hate that about myself—but luckily, I reach past that worst part of me, reach back until I find some kindness.

"You look," I say to Bud Carruthers, "like exactly what you are: 'Boogie in Your Butt' fucking royalty."

"You really do look great," Billie says to him. "Go say hi."

We watch the old man walk off, following the laughter.

For five seconds I make a dumb face that says, *Why are these lives of ours filled with so many slim chances, and why do so many of them break our hearts?*

Five seconds after that, I say to Billie, "Third Eye Blind."

# 12

THEY MADE ME LEAVE NORWAY. I needed a new guardian, and I was a person meeting another person who happened to look like my dead mother, maybe she was her, maybe she'd come back to raise me right. I was a person standing in front of this mother mirror, this copy, this impostor, this reflection, this lip sync, this CGI, this cheap tattoo, this photoshopped goddess, this wild doppelgänger, this eclipse, this dream come true, this nightmare—

I'd landed.

At the airport in San Francisco.

Met by my mother's twin at baggage claim.

But then she said, "This is the afterlife, James," the very first thing she spoke to me.

Her name was Rebecca. She looked to be made of pigeon bones covered in prosciutto. She wore a maroon wig in a bob. "Did they tell you I'm sick?" Rebecca said to me as we walked down the terminal.

"Yes."

"How sick did they say?"

"Just sick."

"I'm this sick," she said, pulling out a lollipop. "Morphine suckers. They don't give you these for chest colds."

"What's morphine?"

We hit baggage claim to get my Tele, walked to her car, a big convertible. She drove fast and crazy down the highway, ripping in and out of lanes.

"We live in the Lower Haight with a bunch of hag hippies," she said. "They gave me nine months to live—the doctors, not the hag hippies—and that was nine months ago. So do you know what that makes this life?"

"No, what?" I asked.

"Dessert," she said, unwrapping two morphine lollipops, one for her, one for me. "This is a life of dessert, and we'll live it accordingly."

I took a small lick. Cherry. Yum. I popped the sucker in my mouth.

She popped a fresh one in hers, too. She turned the music up, asked if I'd ever heard of the Clash, which my mom had played nonstop on vinyl.

"Joe Strummer is a god," I said, repeating my mother's praises. How many glasses of tequila did I watch her spill on our floor, dancing to the Clash? And how did I wish to see her do it one more time? Even crappy parents could play you music that changed your life. It was possible to do both those things in one life: play a kid the Clash; die falling off a bar.

Rebecca seemed impressed that I knew Strummer. "How old are you exactly?"

"Fifteen."

"You're so big."

"Tron and I worked hard."

"How tall are you?"

"Six-five."

"Christ, and you're still growing."

A long pause.

"I never liked your dad." She pulled her sucker out and held it up, waiting, until I cheers'd hers with mine. "But we're going to get along just fine, smart boy," she said, laughing, licking her lollipop, and doing ninety in the slow lane.

We lived with the hippies in a condemned Victorian. Mom Jon, she owned the place, or had, since 1961. The city had written her letters saying the building wasn't safe, offering to buy the property. Those transmissions went unanswered. Then the city wrote letters saying she had no choice now, she had to leave, the property was condemned, she was trespassing, and these letters made Mom Jon howl. They'd been arguing the case in court for years. "Drag me out," she said, a warrior if I'd ever known one. She fought for her home.

Mom Jon threw poetry parties on the top floor. The stage was a pile of dirt that she'd hauled back from Nepal. "Blessed dirt," she told me later. "You read poems from sacred hilltops so they can fly off in the wind."

But I didn't know there was anything special about this dirt when Rebecca and I first got back to the Victorian, straight from the airport with our lollipops. I only knew that we walked in and there were fifty hippies, snapping, smoking, all watching Mom Jon read poetry from her dirt stage.

My lollipop was gone now, but I didn't remember finishing it, didn't remember my mother or father, didn't remember Olympic Village or Norway; I'd never met a bear, let alone wrestled one; I'd never met a copy of my mom and I'd never been in this body and I didn't know any of these snapping hippies, so why did I love them all, why couldn't I stop hugging them, why couldn't they stop hugging me back, why was there so much love in the room, why was there so much love in the world, it was an impossible quantity, it was an atmosphere, an ocean, an ice continent, a rain forest, an active volcano, a garbage star, it was everything—wait, a garbage star, what's a garbage star?—and these lollipops were incredible, then Mom Jon said to Rebecca, "Is that James?" and she said, "He's here!" and Mom Jon said to me, "Get on up," meaning the dirt stage, and I looked to my aunt, that mother mirror, and asked her, "Can I?" and she said, "Go, it's fine," and the hippies were applauding me, as I started my climb, it didn't look so far up at first, looked like only a few feet to the summit, but it was work, it was much farther, I'd been at it for hours, the terrain hard to keep my footing, but nothing would stop my progress, a hundred thousand steps later, I saw Mom Jon smiling at me from the peak, reaching out to help me with this last, almost sheer part of the mountain, and our hands locked, and she pulled me up, brought me next to her, on the sacred dirt, in a condemned Victorian, with all the snapping hippies, welcome home, happy home, and what the hell's a garbage star anyway?

ᚦ

Dusty had on handcuffs now, and his ankles were duct-taped together. We were on little Alcatraz, sitting in the marina.

Dust sat in a chair, and I was inches from his face.

"Can I say something before you finish threatening me?" he asked.

"For old time's sake, sure."

"Because I knew you were at the gig, I knew where you weren't."

"Okay, where *weren't* I?"

"Sound Check," said Dusty. "Wes returned Trick's band's gear."

"Why would he do that?"

"A gesture of good faith."

"Like a Christian waving around their little Bible, stealing Norway with bullshit gifts."

Dusty looked confused. You probably are, too. I clarified:

"Feign good faith and take what you really want."

"All I can tell you," he said, "is that their gear is back. That's the truth."

I knew Dusty so well that I could tell when he was lying, and this was the truth. Was he right when he said I should just let all this go and walk away? It didn't seem right to get safe now. Without consequences, Wes would keep scamming bands, holding Amy hostage.

It did seem right to get Dusty off the board for a minute. I didn't need him around when I finally got my hands on Wes.

"I'm going to let you go," I said to Dusty. "I'll drop you off at emergency, and all I need you to do is tell Wes where we're meeting."

"He won't want to give you home field advantage."

"He won't. Let's meet at Stink Phinger. Two a.m."

Dusty thought for a beat, then nodded. "I think he'll do that. Let's end this before anyone else gets hurt."

"Says the nine-fingered man."

"Wes is like you," he said. "Wes won't quit."

Þ

Amy had an idea. It was wild and, some might say, demented. It was definitely illegal. But it had a certain je ne sais quoi, a kind of antihero swagger that made the idea gleam.

We stood in her houseboat's living room. Dusty, the nine-fingered man, all taped up sitting in a chair, while two matchsticks were still on the floor in front of us, minding their own business.

Meanwhile, Jesse was crashed out in Amy's bed, sweating and venting to devils. Wes wasn't going to kill him today, but Jesse would wish we had, working through the carnival doom of withdrawal.

"Look," said Amy, "if somebody told me what I'm about to tell you, Saint, I'd be shit-talking them in my head. I'd start shit-talking almost as soon as they started flapping gums—so I know that what I'm about to say sounds dumb, but here goes. This day with Jesse has been fun. Fun with a junkie who only speaks in tongues and pukes. He can't even remember my name. He's asked it a hundred times today. But something's happening to me—and it's because of taking care of him. Holy shit, it's changed me. I know! Roll your fucking eyes, but it has! It's the first time since getting into bed with Wes that I was doing something that felt nice—something that made me feel good."

Her mind was firing so fast that she couldn't sit still, so she weaved around her living room, moving around the matchsticks, circling them.

"You're getting a little break," I said.

"What's a little break?"

"Never mind," I said. "Please keep going."

"I want to burn it all down, scorch that whole life I was living. And I want to take care of people. To clarify, I'm using Jesse as an analogy. I don't want to take care of a petting zoo full of withdrawing junkies all day. Gross. That would be fucking awful. I'm using Jesse as an example of doing something for somebody else and not only thinking about myself, thinking what I can get out of a situation and not even caring if I'm making somebody else's life worse. I don't want to be that anymore, Saint, and therefore, I want to set my boat on fire."

That wasn't something you heard very often. There was an island in me that was tickled by her violent poetry, but most of me knew not to be seduced by such cheap magic. It was a trick and a trap. So I had to understand why she needed to torch her own home.

"Why would you burn your houseboat?" I asked Amy.

"These guys," she said, kicking one of the matchsticks, "they tried to kill you."

"That's true."

"We can agree that they should pay for their crimes," she said, sounding like an inspired prosecutor, "and there's a way we do that, and I get enough money to start my new life."

Okay, that last part sounded less like a prosecutor.

"I'm listening," I said.

"They should do time—they should be held accountable for trying to kill you. So we pin it on them. We burn the boat. Stick them back in the Caddy. Call 911 that they were seen fleeing the scene. I get the insurance money. They go to prison. Everyone gets what they want."

The matchsticks were now mumbling behind their blanket-muzzles, sounds I could only assume were in dissent. It was an odd cocktail, her idea. On one hand, Amy was talking about trying to leave an old life behind, one stained with malice, so she could try living on the sunny side of the street—and yet on the other hand, she wanted to frame these guys for arson.

And I thought, *We all live in the moral mud.*

We all feed on the empty calories of rationalizations. If she was asking my consent to pin a crime on some cats, she picked the right ones. The tweaker and the big guy had done nothing to earn any allegiance from me, and this seemed like a solution that would save me from hurting them further myself. So I agreed to help Amy, because it was her boat, and if she wanted to burn it, she should be allowed—and in so doing fucking an insurance company and framing the men who wanted me dead—this wasn't a difficult pill to gag down.

Pilot lights set to spew gas.

Cleaning solvents dumped all over the floor.

Gasoline spilled all over her kitchen table.

Splashed a cologne hit of gas on the matchstick men, too, so the cops could smell.

A candle placed in the center of that table, waiting to be lit, this wick.

I carried Jesse out to the Reliant built during the Louisiana Purchase and laid him down in the back. I put Dusty in the trunk—the day fast becoming rich in human trafficking—and then I untied the matchsticks and limped them up to the Caddy. They got in, sort of conscious, absolutely busted up. I stood at the driver's door, which was open, and they looked up at me.

"We're calling the cops," I said, "and you're their number one suspect."

"We are?" the big guy said.

"You are."

"For what exactly?" he woozily asked.

"For burning down Amy's boat."

"We did that? Huh. It seems like the kind of act you'd remember committing."

They stopped talking and, from the Caddy, stared at the marina with confused faces. They could see the houseboat was fine.

"But there's just one thing," said the big guy. "The boat's not on fire."

"It is."

"It is?"

"Yes."

"But it's not," he said.

"We're lighting it up right now. Good luck out there. The cops will be coming and you smell like gasoline," I said, sniffing the air.

The tweaker really wanted to say something, but the broken vacuum he called a jaw wouldn't cooperate. The big guy didn't have anything to add to the conversation, simply driving the Caddy off.

I was going to miss that Caddy. It was a terrific shit-box.

I stood in the parking lot for a minute.

The glass birds were with me, cawing, crazy, agitated, agreeable.

"This is sort of nice, huh?" I said to the birds.

"Who are you talking to?" Dusty yelled from the Reliant's trunk.

"Not you," I said, then to the birds: "I'm glad you're here. Should we go burn her boat?"

They agreed, those incredible bastards.

I came back on the boat, and the murder followed, coming in the windows, wings flapping, claws gripping the chairs, tables, and lamps that they landed on, me looking up and the whole houseboat had hundreds of my father's birds, but they were somehow real—both glass *and* animated—shining impossible light through their bodies, but with blinking eyes and moving bodies jutting up and down where they stood.

Amy and I stood right next to the wick.

Standing by the fuse, her new future.

"I'm assuming you want to do the honors," I said to her.

"You bet your ass," she said.

Amy lit the wick on the candle that was turned on its side, and we walked outside, untying the ropes, the boat slowly drifting away from the marina.

We stood on the dock, watching for a few minutes, until that first burst of orange shone through the boat's window.

A fireball erupted on the water, floating away from us.

The glass birds and I were lucky enough to see Amy's old life immolate.

I wanted to believe that the next Amy was going to be the best yet.

ᚠ

Rebecca and I were high on morphine lollipops, laughing, riding the bus around SF. Our favorite was the 22 Filmore, but we rode all over town, knew the routes backward and forward. Still, we hopped on the 22 most often. Rarely did we have anywhere to go. She wanted to be outside, and she had trouble walking now.

There were no more treatments left for her.

Or there were, but she was done with them.

"Chemo might be killing some of the cancer," she said, "but it's also killing the rest of me. I'm not living like that no more."

So we rode the bus. I was a person and she was a person and these lollipops were people, and we sat in our seats, on this bus, on this tropical island, this view from the top of the Andes, how the world appeared a hundred feet down in the ocean, a motorcycle ripping through windy countryside roads, we were a chandelier, a classic car, an emerald necklace, a bacon cheeseburger—

Wait.

Right.

We were riding public transportation.

"I pretend buses are big limousines," she said. "But also better than a limo, because we're surrounded by lunatics."

It was true. On the 22 people were arguing, kissing, crying, playing music too loud, flirting, panhandling, preaching, stealing, withdrawing, shoving, fighting, commuting, going to school, going to the dentist, the doctor; there were brides and grooms, grooms and grooms, brides and brides; there were parties, musical guests—I even saw a girl go into labor in the back. The whole bus waited for an ambulance to take her away. Once they left, we cheered.

"Why would you want to be alone in a limousine?" she asked. "Me, I always prefer the company of the mentally ill."

I'd been living with her and Mom Jon for eight months. Celebrated a birthday with them. I took care of Rebecca, and by that I mean I sat with her on the living room couch, watching old Cassavetes movies, playing her songs on my Tele. She wouldn't let me do more for her than that, hissing at me, "Don't take my agency, goddamn it."

I respected that.

Soon, though, it wouldn't be an option.

Weak and sleepy.

Wasn't eating much.

But more than any of that it was a certain look creeping into her eyes, like they were changing lenses, getting ready to see the next world.

"I talked to Mom Jon about you," she said. "Once I'm gone, you pay your share, of course. But my room is yours."

"How am I going to pay?"

"You'll need to figure that out."

"Should I go back to school?"

"Anything you need to learn is on this bus," she said.

"I mean a high school diploma."

"I'm going to leave."

"You don't know that—don't know when."

"That's not what I mean. I want to tell you what today is," she said to me. "Today isn't the day I die. Today is the day I get off the bus."

"Of course, you're not going to die today."

"You're not hearing me. Those are our only two options: you watch me die, or you watch me get off a bus. And I won't have you watching me die. So today, I'm getting off the bus."

"I don't mind watching you die."

"You've already seen too much."

"I can help."

"It's a better end to our story. Not the day I died. No way. The day you watched me get off the bus. A better memory for you," she said. "You'll always see me smiling at you, walking off the bus for a final time. There's love in my eyes. You can see it."

The bus pulled into the next stop. She stood up and motioned for me to stay.

I startled, and my feet got numb: "You mean now?!"

"You can take care of yourself," she said. "I know it. Sell my things. Keep the money. And there's a pillowcase full of lollipops in the closet."

She walked toward the exit.

She was going to get off the bus.

That was something I was going to see.

On the day you were born, the gods gave you an empty cemetery, and until you died, you had to endure watching that cemetery fill with everyone you ever loved—what an unbearable predicament, knowing these bodies would fall—all the joy in their hearts fertilizing the earth—and I thought, *What a stiff bill it was to feel.*

These cemeteries, these cities, inside us!

I wasn't ready to watch a woman who looked exactly like my mother leave. I asked her, "What if we do this tomorrow instead? Please? One more day together? Please? Just one more?"

She stopped walking toward the exit and looked at me. "What's one more day going to do?"

"Give me what my parents never did," I said. "Give me one more day. All I want is knowing there can be one more day with you. Please."

She sighed, came back, crashed next to me.

She picked her teeth without a care, asked, "So how are we going to spend this last day?"

Þ

She couldn't rest that night. She was so uncomfortable lying on her bony back that sleep was next to impossible. She smoked two whole joints, and I played Otis Redding records. At one point, she started crying, and when I asked what I could do to help, she said, "All you need to do is let me get off the bus."

"Okay," I said, "tomorrow, for sure."

It wasn't what I wanted to say. But the only thing that felt worse in that moment than agreeing to say goodbye was begging her to stay— not that it would've mattered. Her mind was made up. She was heading out.

That was tomorrow, however, and now, right as she was passing out for the night, I woke Mom Jon up, told her what Rebecca planned to do—and that I needed her help to plan something.

"What am I getting myself into?" asked Mom Jon.

"We are going to send her off right," I said, and told Mom Jon what I wanted to do.

She nodded along, impressed. "You're all right," she said. "Most kids are bullshit, but I really like you."

Even though it was late, we got on the horn, alerted the hippies. We'd need their help. The next morning, Mom Jon was out the door early to line everything up for the other part of the plan.

Around noon, Rebecca and I came to the bus stop to catch our favorite 22. Rebecca stared at it as it slowed, stopped, and we walked on. She didn't understand what she saw: It was entirely empty—the whole bus—and that had never happened before.

"Is there a bomb on here or something?" Rebecca asked the driver, climbing on.

"Something," the driver said, laughing, and she had a little pink lipstick on her teeth. "Something better than a bomb."

We made our way down the aisle, and I said, "Today, it really is like a limousine. You've got the place to yourself."

Rebecca frowned at that: "I told you I like riding this bus because we *aren't* alone."

At the next block, the bus pulled over for another stop.

"Maybe we're not," I said.

And here came the hippies, all smiles, all snapping, paying their fares and storming aboard. Mom Jon was the last one on, the final person to come up to Rebecca and pay their respects: "I hear we're sending you on a voyage." Mom Jon looked at me. "At least that's what he told me when he set this all up for you."

Rebecca grabbed me by the cheeks and brought me in. She heaved with tears while she showered me in smooches. "You did this for me?" she asked.

"This bus will take you to Valhalla," I said.

"I'll take your word for it," she said, and I was still in her arms, still feeling her lips on my cheeks, my forehead. Then she whispered something simply for me: "They gave you this life because you can take it—you can take it, and you'll still go on to do extraordinary things."

Did you hear that?

There used to be someone who thought I could amount to something.

"Someone put on the music!" a hippie shouted.

And there he was, Iggy Pop, serenading us on our bus, talking coolly about nightclubbing. We all knew the words and danced in the aisle of the bus, and the driver with lipstick on her teeth didn't squawk at all, us all dancing in circles.

Could you understand that?

The driver blew by every stop now that we filled the bus, laughing to herself as she sped by people trying to flag her down, cussing at her. "This feels good!" she said to us. "I should do this at least once a week."

I wanted you to board this bus with us, wanted you to see the joy in which we began her voyage. Wanted you to hear us sing and witness this god-awful dancing, the whole bus a zooming club. I needed you to know that there was a day in my life when somebody believed that I might be extraordinary, and though that would never be true—it didn't matter.

She said it.

And I heard it.

And yes, I had to watch her walk off the bus in a matter of minutes, and yes, that was going to happen, and yes, there wasn't anything I could do about it.

I couldn't save her.

She didn't want to die in front of me.

And that made me love her.

Though I was going to be alone.

Though I was the last of my kind.

Fenrir the monstrous wolf.

So I was telling you everything about this last bus ride, and I hope this next decision doesn't offend you, but you aren't invited to ride with us any longer. You need to get off here. Our scene will roll on, releasing Rebecca into the wild, but this is your stop.

You need to go.

Why?

Because I don't want you to see these last minutes; they were only ours. Only for us.

And you won't see the moment where she walked off and away and lived a few more weeks until we got the call that she had passed.

She was a mother mirror, and mothers knew only how to leave me.

So here was where she hopped off.

You don't get to see how I sobbed, watching her slowly limping away down the street. I was trying hard to be an adult in this moment, but all I wanted to do was run to her, scream that I didn't care if it was going to be difficult to watch her die—I just couldn't bear my mother's face leaving again. I didn't care if I was her nurse and chef and maid and minister, didn't care at all, no, I'd be whatever she needed, I'd convert to whatever god would keep her here—if only she'd turn around, board the bus, come home . . .

None of those things, however, are for you. I shouldn't have mentioned them.

And so you hopped off right as we were dancing to Iggy, right as Mom Jon spun me around ballroom style. The hippies had their arms up in all sorts of slow, serpentine patterns, and they smiled like huldras. We were all swept up in a ride that would never end, no such things as diseases—and buses never ran out of gas—and the human heart was a garbage star.

# 13

DUSTY AND I were out front of the emergency room. I'd taken off his handcuffs, cut loose his legs, and he flexed his feet to get their circulation back. He was in the passenger seat, and I was behind the wheel—our opposite posts from when we used to work together in his cab.

"Here," I said, fishing in my pocket and handing him his finger. "It hasn't been that long. I bet they can fix it."

"Can I say something before I go?" he asked. "I want to give you a compliment."

Dusty held his severed finger in his hand and used it like a character in some sort of cannibal stage play.

"This is me," he said of the finger.

"How much blood have you lost?" I asked.

"Most of it, probably," said Dusty, "but what I'm saying isn't inspired by blood loss. No, it's grief."

He used the severed finger to scratch at his dustache.

We both started laughing, very hard, at the concept of scratching your face with an amputated finger, and for a moment we were two friends back in Dusty's cab, another night at our speeding office, and we weren't here in front of the emergency room with his chewed-off digit.

Dusty held the finger close to me, then had it march off theatrically. "All I had to do was choose the right thing earlier," he said. "All I had to do was be like you." He planted the finger so it stood straight up on the Reliant's dashboard. "So now that's me. Up there, alone."

I pointed to the dash. "That's not sanitary."

"No, I don't suppose it is," he said. "Maybe they fix my finger, maybe not. But I lost you today, Saint, and there isn't anything to be done about that."

"You lost yourself," I said, "and take it from me: You're the only person who can get him back." I retrieved his lonely finger from up on the dashboard and handed it back to him.

He held the finger in an open palm. "So there's hope?" he said, crawling from the car.

"Only one way to find out."

Watching Dusty walk toward the emergency room, I felt a bit like Denis, right at the end, knowing he'd see for only another burp of time. I was witnessing an image that would be nice to take with me into the darkness, if I never saw Dusty again.

He had said something I couldn't ever forget: "I lost you today, Saint," and in that moment I knew that I loved Dusty.

Love could come up and bite you at all kinds of absurd times. And in a way, that was my favorite thing about love: the cruelty of its spontaneity and its droughts.

There went Dusty, moving through the hospital's front doors, heading inside to learn if he'd ever be whole again.

ᛈ

After that, I went home. It had been a long one, and part of me wished I could call it a day, crash in my cozy punk house. But I couldn't, the job wasn't done. And as I pulled up and stomped the brakes, tires squealing, I quickly realized I may never be able to—the roof of our home blazed, black smoke wafting into the night.

Since I was coming from one fire, it was pretty odd to end up at another. And yet there it was. Most days, our lives had zero fires, but today, it seemed like everything was ready to burn.

For a moment, I looked on in wonder, even as my adrenaline loosened up its muscles, getting ready to go.

In our warehouse's second-floor windows, there were people inside. The room wasn't burning, not yet, but they were trapped and pounding the windows. A calm settled over me. It was all the training, all the fights. When the world went mad, I set my temper to simmer. At the same time, the ancestors squatting in my bloodstream rowed their dragon ships faster, as if they themselves were returning home after months on the ocean, only to see their village lustrous on the horizon, flames lighting their houses to supernovas, collapsing homes and barns, their families somewhere inside these husks, and all they could do was beg the gods, promise them crops and opulent worship—songs, stories, legends, poems, punk rock—anything they wanted, as they rowed faster in their ships—these boats in my bloodstream—rowing with me toward our burning home, leaping onto the shore, and running up the beach.

Toward our families.

Toward this place that we thought was our future but was being incinerated, and all we had left was hot dirt. We were just cold warriors, more exhausted than you could imagine, muscles aching, eating next to nothing, a speck of salted fish, a swig of sour milk—a pack of malnourished wolves, these Vikings.

Wait.

I needed to get my head out of my bloodstream.

I needed to be here.

And what I meant by that was this: I needed to run into the building that was on fire.

Most of my housemates were out front, hands on heads, crying, shaking, sooty, perplexed. Some had boxes and things they grabbed in that panicked instant when it dawned on them that they were about to lose everything—and that was such a wrong concept, everything you owned, burned up—that was so impossible to process in that instant that you snatched the most random things: a fedora, panties, a pair of Docs, vinyl. One guy had a toaster oven; another had his bowling ball.

After calling 911, they had no idea what anyone should do, though they knew that somebody should do something—brave, brazen, dumb—and so they shouted their prayers for aid into the unhelpful air.

"Someone needs to help them!" a housemate said to another. There must have been a gig in our upstairs venue. Dozens of people.

We peered up to the second floor, where I could still see people in the smoky room.

"The stairs are blocked, and they can't get the windows open," another of my housemates said, the one holding the toaster oven.

"Where have you been, J—"

"Don't call me that," I interrupted.

"What do we—"

"Shut up."

"But we—"

I tired of this productive chat, and so I sprinted into the burning building.

The smell was stunning, the simple intensity. It never occurred to me before that you could smell intensity, that it had not only a temperature but an odor. A stink.

Some animal armpit.

Rank, sexual.

Being in a fire that was destroying your home was fighting a mythological beast, and I knew that there was no point in trying to save the structure, our various art cages were kindling, mostly. The wiring in the building was like twenty-year-old guitar strings, and I just assumed that one exploded from overuse—that must've started the blaze—and that lone spark metastasized, made friends, these sparks were having the time of their lives and these sparks grew from hatchlings to dragons, and they crackled and flung fire from their mouths, hissed warnings at all of us, and I could go no farther than the bottom of the staircase, which had a fire raging at its top, impossible to get to the people on the second floor, though I could hear them screaming for help.

It was all going to be gone soon—and I hadn't even come here to save anyone. I'd returned for my bow, which I wanted with me in my showdown with Wes. Problem was it didn't seem like there was time to save both the people and my bow, which was not just a weapon, not just mine, but Tron's, and I didn't have many possessions of his left, and I didn't want our bow to burn up like his book did, year after year. I screamed.

How many fires had scattered my father's life through the heavens?

I couldn't stomach another piece of him leaving.

So:

I gazed around the burning room.

Then I saw it: the crow's nest. I dashed to its ladder, and I shook it with everything that I had, shook it free from the nails holding it in place, and I pried it free, and the crow's nest above crashed to the ground, and I hauled the ladder, which was incredibly heavy, but I muscled it outside.

Finally, when the work was almost over, those spectating housemates helped me the last twenty feet to set the ladder on the ground right below the window. All those animal crawls. All those pull-ups. Those rounds wrestling with the bear. They were training for moments like this, because I had the body control and strength of a gymnast.

We planted the ladder, and I climbed up to the second floor. I knew why they couldn't get the windows open—they'd been installed right-side out—so once I was up there, I flipped the latch that was supposed to be inside. Smoke poured out. Once it cleared, I saw that they were losing their minds in there. People crossing over. People who had accepted their fates. They knew it; they were dead. They had no past, and the next few beats of their heart were the only things they had left.

Finally, life was precious.

Finally, we knew how to care.

Too bad we needed to be in a burning building to accept what a joy it was to be alive.

And now it registered in their startled brains that I'd opened the window—and now came the people stampede.

"Slow down," I told them. "You'll all get out."

I cleared myself from their path by balancing myself on the pipes and wires on the building's wall.

My housemates held the ladder, while I held on to the outside of the window frame with one hand, using the other to help people out and shimmy down. I counted as they came out, thirty-six of them, yes, thirty-six of them who almost burned. Thirty-six who could have lost their lives tonight, but now, they were all making it out . . .

I know that we aren't the only ones of us, and yes, I know that sounds confusing, but here's what I mean: other universes. There are others, our mirrors, who live in their own universes, who have their own West Oaklands, own punk houses. And as I helped my friends out the window I witnessed the glorious sweat of their relief and their death-defying gazes. Maybe in these other universes, it isn't the night I come to get my bow. Or I did it an hour earlier. It's possible that in those warehouses, maybe they aren't so lucky. And my friends are lost, daughters and sons, mothers and fathers, siblings, surrogate sisters and brothers.

And the fire in those universes spreads faster. One minute they're in a room made of music, and suddenly, the walls go up and they're in the maw of a monster.

In these other universes, a band is playing. Maybe punk or hip-hop or jazz. Or a DJ. The room is going off, the energy, the high, and then you smell smoke. And in these universes, fire follows, and there's no way out—and we have to say goodbye to these light elves, these friends who can still live forever if we fan their story—if we tattoo their memory—if we make them transcendent. Infamous. Unforgettable.

Maybe their names were:

Cash.

Jonathan.

Em.

Barrett.

David.

Micah.

Billy.

Chelsea.

Feral.

Alex.

Michela.

Nick.

Sara.

Travis.

Johnny.

Ara.

Donna.

Amanda.

Edmond.

Griffin.

Casio.

Jason.

Draven.

Jennifer.

Maybe another Jennifer.

Vanessa.

Wolfgang.

Hanna.

Benjamin.

Nicole.

Michele.

Another Jennifer.

Alex.

Peter.

Nick.

Chase.

Or maybe those aren't their names.

Or maybe they didn't need names now. Those letters that meant something here were useless as they made their way into the sky, to the parties in Valhalla. Bands to hear. There was a stage made of ice where the music always blared, off-key, speeding up and slowing down, botched chords, broken strings, thrashed amps, hoarse throats, the wunjo of punk rock.

And if I could say something to the people in those other universes who had to say goodbye to those they loved, may the scribbles on this page whisper into your ear: *We won't ever let them die, we won't ever let them die, we won't ever let them die . . .*

But in my universe, after all thirty-six light elves made it out of the burning room, it was my turn to scramble down, too, and yet I didn't.

Instead I climbed into the fire.

Yeah, I rocketed into the second-story window. Moved to the door on the far side of the room, to where the fire was dissolving the stairs. I jumped up for an exposed pipe, and I shimmied above the fire toward the back of the warehouse. If my hands slipped, I'd fall and burn alive.

But I had to see about our bow, our shield.

I wasn't going to say adios to the last few things I had from Tron, besides my happy monster.

I was on the pipe, coughing, tears leaking down my face from my one good eye.

I was sweaty and I could barely see anything except the pipe above my head, but there came that feeling again—joy.

Joy!

I kept shimmying and coughing and crying, and it didn't feel like there was any place else to be, didn't feel like there was any other way to say it except this: I was a person who dangled above the underworld, a cauldron of lava beneath me as I tempted this near death.

I was two art cages away from mine, and both had fires going in them, but neither ecosystem had been leveled yet. Some things were burning, sure, while others were not. There was still hope for the bow, though my palms were getting scalded on the pipe and visibility approached zero.

Finally I was above my own cage. The bow was under my bed. The shield, on the wall. Another two minutes and it would all be gone. These last bits of Tron.

I dropped into my room and got the shield down, jimmied the bow out and put it across my back so I had one burned hand free—a huge blister forming on the palm—and the other had my shield.

It was time, I knew, to run through a wall.

Now, the walls between our art cages were just drywall, so making it through those would be easy, but there were rolling doors in the back that hadn't rolled in years, which would be a much harder barrier to crash through.

So:

You know what you call a Viking hopped up on adrenaline in a moment of mortal emergency?

A berserker.

And that was what I became.

The man-monster that could run through fire and splinter walls.

I screamed, cried, cawed with the power of a thousand glass birds; I had the shield up to protect my face and I sprinted, sprinted, sprinted—

—through one wall, one cage—

I sprinted, sprinted, sprinted—

—through the next wall, the next cage—

and the only thing that was left was the stuck-down rolling door, and I found even more blood for my muscles. I'd never run as fast as I was going now, the rolling doors fifteen feet ahead, the fire all around, the fire was going to take whatever it wanted,

the fire was irrational,

greedy with its pillaging,

and the fire made it clear that it was going to take me down, too—but I had a shield, and I had something to say about the outcome of this scrape.

Assuming I was running fast enough.

Assuming the shield was strong enough.

Assuming I put every ounce of my 280 pounds behind it.

And I yelled again, eye wide, every longship in my bloodstream putting as much wind in their sails as possible, and we were just one more step away, one more step from the rolling door,

the wall we needed to crash through,

it couldn't simply be me,

no,

I needed their strength,

all of theirs,

all those ghosts and

all their gales of suffering—

they could make more wind,

more speed, and

then we were there—

we were velocity and joy,

how a shield hits a rolling door,

how a shoulder and back slam into a solid object,

how my brain got bobbled all around in the collision,

how at that moment of impact one of us would fall—

because that was how all fights ended:

a victor,

a casualty,

the fire,

a man,

a boundary,

we'd know soon enough,

either you got out and lived,

or you stayed in Hel, and

I hit that wall with all I had—

# WHOLE FOODS HALLUCINATION

THAT WAS A TONGUE. It felt waffle-wide and was in need of a glass of water. Maybe two. And somebody was running it up and down my face. My eye was closed, and I couldn't remember the command to make its door swing up. It seemed so simple, opening your eyes, but I was baffled.

"You're a dreadful prophet dancing on broken glass," said a man, who must have been connected to the tongue.

That was the logical thing, I thought.

I was yelling at my eye, screaming at that no good, no opening bead. But I was blind like Denis. One minute you had one, then every direction, pitch black.

I got licked again.

"You're a prophet who broke the glass before dancing on it," this poetic tongue said. "Now why would you do that? That's the question, yeah? It's what I want to know, what I need to know. Why, man? Spill it."

This tongue had questions.

And was sorta bossy.

But who was in charge of teaching a tongue some manners in the first place?

These were existential questions.

Also, I couldn't remember where I was.

Also, there were patterns on the back of my eyelid that looked like pink clouds pinwheeling.

And my body, much like my eye, was disinterested in responding to my calls of motion and gesture.

Oh well.

At least I had this tongue to keep me company.

Another batch of licks.

Then a sigh from the tongue's rightful owner. Then he said, "Hey, man, there's something you should know."

"What?"

"My dog is licking your face."

*Huh,* I thought, *that was surprising news.*

So I said, "Huh. That's surprising news."

"I can imagine."

"How did I get here?"

"We were sitting here minding our own business, and you crashed through the wall."

"Where is here?"

"Whole Foods."

"That's also surprising."

"You're telling us. One minute, there wasn't a hole in the wall. Then you made your . . . elaborate entrance."

"Is Billie here?"

"I am Billie."

"And why's your dog licking me?"

"He's friendly," Billie said, "and I was hoping it might wake you up."

"How long did he lick me before I came to?"

"That's a you-think-you-wanna-know-but-really-don't topic."

More licks on my face.

"Seems very friendly," I said.

"Don't you think it's odd that a dog shares ninety-eight percent of its DNA with wolves?" Billie asked.

I commanded my eye to open. Finally, it felt like listening.

But perhaps not at the most advantageous time.

For sitting right next to me was that dog, a Norwegian buhund. That in and of itself was a good thing. I loved battle hounds. But Billie's hound had a hard dick pointing at me, bright red, the color of fresh rhubarb.

We were at Billie's check stand. He was behind it. I lay on the floor, the dog sitting next to me. Nobody else was in the store.

"I want to set your mind at ease," Billie said, pointing at the dog's rhubarb rocket giving me the eye. "What's happening south of the border has nothing to do with you."

"I'm glad to hear that."

"Where's Trick Wilma?"

"I had to leave her at Gilman."

"Was she upset about that?"

"I don't know yet," I said, "but I'm assuming so."

"You played the show and bolted?!" Billie was laughing at me now. "Oh yeah, she's gonna kick your ass."

"How did I get here again?"

"You crashed through the wall."

"Right. I don't remember doing that."

"What's the last thing you remember?"

"Flying above a village on fire."

"You should stop doing things like that," said Billie. "Stop for her. For you. Don't go down this road and get locked up again."

"I was flying for good. I was saving people from a dragon. You know what?" I said. "It's not so bad in Whole Foods."

"It can get a bit boring. And at times, I get anxious, knowing everything wild I'm missing outside these walls. A Whole Foods life is a prison, too."

"A good prison?"

"The best."

"How do I get back to where I came from?" I asked.

"You head back through your hole, I'd imagine," he said.

I looked over to where the front doors were supposed to be, but they weren't there. Only walls all around the whole joint. No official entrance or exit. Only the damage I'd caused, a dark wound to the outside.

Since my eye was back online, I tried the legs, the arms, and thankfully, I found myself ambulatory again. I sat up and gazed at Billie and his buhund, the rhubarb rocket still in full salute.

"Can I give you some advice?" Billie said.

"Why not?"

"Find Trick. The sooner, the better."

"You've made your position clear on that—and are on the verge of getting preachy."

"You have a chance, Saint, a chance to choose something good."

"I've already chosen," I said, "but I'm finishing things with Wes." I hopped up, shook Billie's hand, pet the dog's head, and continued speaking over my shoulder as I walked off toward the hole I'd made in the wall: "Once that's done, I'll be able to see you again."

I stopped and looked back; Billie rubbed the dog's head and they stared at me.

"I hope so," said Billie.

I couldn't find the right words, so I walked to my hole in the wall. I wanted to say something about the beauty of helping other people get out of a burning building—about how risking your life was the purest way to live it.

Then I crawled through my hole in Whole Foods's wall and disappeared.

# 14

"**GET OFF ME!**" I said, sitting up, startled. I was behind our burning warehouse, lying in the gravel by the dumpster. This stray had licked my face, brought me back as I heard sirens pinging my ears. The dog backed up, unsure, and we eyeballed each other.

My shield lay next to me, splintered beyond repair. I thanked it for getting me out alive.

I walked toward the front of the building. It was chaos, a population of coughing people. All my housemates were still there, watching the fire, lamenting all they'd lost, shock lacquering faces into strange masks. And it also looked like most of the rescued heads from the show upstairs had stuck around, too, milling about, trying to make sense of this.

Or they just wanted to watch the building burn.

It would be kind of gorgeous if we weren't losing everything.

My housemates called to me. Did I want to process or talk about my feelings? They were thankful I showed up when I did. But I was in a hurry, had my bow and that was what I needed for what was next.

I went to Got Jokes's 1791 Reliant, fired up the engine, drove down the block. My head was killing me, but besides my blistered palms, I was all right.

A firetruck turned in front of me, splashing the wastewater air with colored ripples, blues and reds.

It was pretty if you didn't breathe.

ᛈ

I called Dusty in the ER from the road, 12:30 a.m., speeding through Oakland back to Stink Phinger. I needed to get there with as much time to spare. All the supplies I needed were in place. Amy and Jesse were already at the club, in her office. It was almost time to bring this invader named Wes down, this fucking Christian coming to Norway selling his little god, a thief pimping a thief.

"What's the word?" I asked Dusty.

"He's in."

"I was asking about your finger."

"Oh."

"I'm going to ask about Wes, too, obviously," I said, "but I was starting with you as we navigate this difficult time in our relationship."

"It's been a day that favors the unfortunate," he said, "and in that spirit, my finger remains unattached."

"Why?"

"It turns out that I should have been championing two things above all else: keeping the finger clean and keeping it cold."

"So no dustache scratching or sticking it up on the filthy dashboard?"

"In hindsight, these were the actions of a fool," he said.

I wasn't going to argue hygiene with him. "So what's happening?" I asked.

"They are pumping me full of everything to stave off infection."

"Glad they are looking out for you."

"The human mouth is dirty," he said, "so they are trying to save me from you."

"We are saving each other from each other," I said, and as soon as it was out of my mouth, I thought, *Isn't that our secret mission here?*

"That sounds nicer than you munching off my finger."

"We are saving each other from each other. Say it," I said.

"We are saving each other from each other," said Dusty.

"I'm hoping they can put it back on."

"They said reattachment is much more difficult if the whole finger has been lost—and you bit at the base."

"I was prioritizing detachment."

"There is plenty of blame to go 'round," he said.

"And Wes?"

"He'll be there at two. But he won't be alone, and he won't fight fair."

"That," I said, "makes two of us."

Þ

The scene in Amy's office at Stink Phinger: Jesse was crashed on a love seat in the corner, an upside-down umbrella next to him with bile and stomach dregs forming a pond that smelled like bleu cheese.

"An umbrella?" I said to Amy, who sat behind her desk.

"Desperate times," she said.

I scratched Jesse on the scalp as he dreamed of drugs. I didn't even need to ask him what flickered through his brain, because I remembered how the first days of withdrawal loaded me up with starving demons, desperate to eat drugs, their favorite food, their only food— and they weren't going to stop the torture until they were sated. They weren't being unreasonable. All they wanted was to be fat and happy and high. They couldn't understand why you'd cut them off, why you'd sully a good thing, just score, just fix, these demons screamed, and the pain would end. There was no reason to suffer through this abstinence. They knew how to solve the problem.

I rubbed Jesse on the back: "Can you hear me?" I said.

He looked up at me. "Did I eat your eye, or was that a dream?"

"No, that happened."

"Oh," he said, his own eyes shut now, his forehead scrunched up, confused, anguished. He poured sweat. He smelled like sheets that hadn't been washed in a month. "Can you remind me why I ate it?"

"Because it's going to help you."

"Your eye is?"

"Yes."

"How?"

"It's fighting the demons," I said. "Can you feel it?"

"Don't you have demons, too?" he asked. "Don't you need the power of your eye?"

I couldn't make him understand that I no longer needed it. I'd learned how to be roommates with my demons. My mind was its own punk house now, the demons and me. Now it was the eye's turn to help Jesse.

His face relaxed, and watching that dollop of peace smear across him made me forget the day's chaos. It wouldn't last long. I needed to get ready for the battle trance. But I could spare five seconds staring at Jesse like he was an eclipse in the sky. Like he was the moon blocking the sun.

Then that serenity on his face buckled, turned to agony. He was remembering something—and that momentary flash of peace was gone. "Wait. Is it today or tomorrow?" he asked.

"It's always today."

"I mean, if it's tomorrow, Wes is going to kill me today."

"He's not going to kill you at all. Not this today or the next one—and not the today after that."

"That's great news," said Jesse. "Tell your eye thanks."

"Tell it yourself. It's yours now," I said. "You have three."

"That doesn't seem fair," he said. "Are you sure you don't want it back?"

I kissed Jesse on the crown of his head. Maybe there were no big or little breaks. Maybe a life was just the process of breaking over and over.

"It's brutal what you're going through," I said to him, "but it's worth it."

He didn't hear me anymore. How could he? How could he hear anything as the demons roared for food?

"You've been giving him sugar?" I asked Amy.

"I try," she said, "but he's keen on shitting his pants or puking right after."

"Give me the keys to the club."

Amy tossed them to me.

Right then, my phone buzzed. A text from Trick. She was outside.

"The two of you stay in here with the door locked," I said to Amy. "I'll come get you when it's safe."

ᛈ

I went back outside, to the empty street, but it was full of birds. On the sidewalks, on the cars, on the boarded-up strip clubs, on the parking meters up to the powerlines—a thousand glass birds, all carnival colors, glowing, shimmering.

They began shrieking louder than a hard-core set at Gilman. Caws coming through amplifiers, distorted, megaphoned. They sounded, somehow, different from how they ever did before. What were they saying? What did they want me to do? They hopped up and down, their claws clattering on the sidewalk, in a kind of syncopated, tribal performance.

How could I know how to interpret their dance?

They were here to watch the fight. That was the only thing I could come up with. They wanted to watch Wes go down.

Trick leaned against the club's front, smoking, and as soon as she saw me she punched me in face.

I said to her, "I deserve that—and probably one more as well."

She punched me in the face two more times.

"Don't tell me how many times to fucking punch you!" she said. "I'll punch you as many times as I want!"

My gods, this woman.

"You just left?!" she said, punching me a fourth time. "We played the show of shows. You can't just bolt, Saint!"

Fifth punch.

In twenty minutes, Wes would be here. I didn't have much more time to waste being punched.

"We played the set of our lives and you just left," she said, which was accompanied by another fist.

I took a step back and put up my arms: "Are you done?"

"I've been looking for you," she said, trying another punch, but I ducked this one.

"I'm working on your gear, remember?" I said, and opened the trunk, grabbed the bow and arrows. "It's back. In your studio."

It didn't seem like she ingested the good news, instead pointing at my bow. "Why do you have that?"

"We can't stand here," I said. "We need to get in position."

"For what?"

"Did you hear me? Your gear has been returned."

She punched me again. "Well, I really like that," she said.

"I'm sorry I left without saying goodbye."

"I like that you're sorry, too."

"Am I getting back in your good graces?"

"I'm falling in love with you, goddamn it," she said.

My nose was bleeding now from her hands, and I smiled at her. "Please stop punching me," I said.

"Okay," she said, kissing me instead. "I have news."

"Come with me," I said, "and we'll talk."

"Where?"

We ran across the street, pulled down the fire escape on a building, climbed on the roof. Nobody was around who didn't have business here at this time of night. This was as good a place as any.

Trick and I crawled to the edge of the roof. I got the bow and arrows ready to go.

She looked at me. "Tell me you're not killing anyone."

"I'm not."

"Because you can't."

"Okay."

"Do you want to know why you can't?"

"Because you love me," I said.

"Gross, no," she said. "Because Jawbreaker wants us to do the West Coast with them. Twelve shows in two weeks. We leave on Thursday."

"Are you serious?"

"They loved the music, Saint. They said we sound sludgy as fuck."

"They said that?"

"Yes."

"Called us sludgy as fuck?"

"They did."

"Well, that's good news, Trick," I said.

"You can call me Wil. I won't let most people call me that. But you can."

"There are names you abbreviate and names you appreciate," I said, "and if it's all right with you, I'll always call you Trick Wilma."

"No. You're calling me fucking Wil."

I wasn't going to tell her this, but you should know: I would adhere to her wishes and call her Wil when I addressed her directly in dialogue. But in my mind, whenever I thought of her, she'd be Trick Wilma the Valkyrie.

She kissed me again. "We should have sex soon."

"That's a good idea," I said.

Then a car engine. Tires skidding onto the block.

I peeked over the edge of the building's roof, and an old muscle car, a red Barracuda, stopped right in front of the club.

"Okay," I said to her, "he's here."

# 15

A MAN HOPPED OUT of the passenger side. He went up to Stink Phinger's door, tried to open it, shrugged his shoulders.

Then another man, the driver, joined him at the locked door, the closed gate to our village.

They assumed we were all inside, shivering and scared of them, saying our rushed last goodbyes. Frightened animals, they thought.

But I was across the street. I nocked an arrow, aimed.

I hit one of the men in his left hamstring, arrow sticking from his leg.

The other man looked toward my position, facing me, standing right out in the open like that, which seemed an unorthodox strategy of self-protection if you just witnessed someone else being wounded.

I nocked another arrow. He still didn't move, dumbfounded, his friend hollering and pointing to the arrow in his leg and saying repeatedly, "There's an arrow in my leg, there's an arrow in leg, there's an arrow in my leg . . ."

Seemed to me that he shouldn't be the only one participating in this arrow-leg fun, so I drew and shot again, hitting the man staring toward me in his right quad.

"There's an arrow in my leg!" he called, too.

And I thought, *We can get in so over our heads that all we have left is to repeat the facts of our suffering.*

"There's an arrow in my leg!" they called together.

"Stay here," I said to Trick.

"You have so many problems," she said, and I took off and flew down the fire escape, stormed across the street. There was only one other person in the back of their car, and it had to be Wes.

I took the hitter-quitter out and I had the angle, would see if he reached for a gun, but he just sat there, didn't even turn to face me, hadn't moved, statue still, and I smashed the Barracuda's window with the hitter-quitter and shoved my hand inside and grabbed the head by the hair and it came off in my hand, the whole head. It required a beat of interpretation, holding the severed mannequin cranium as it swayed.

I was hypnotized, for just moment. Lost my edge, my guard—so when the trunk rocketed open, he had the drop on me. A man stood straight up from the trunk, pumped a shotgun, pointed it right at me.

I let the hitter-quitter clank on the pavement. I dropped the head, too, like it was spoiled fruit. The man with the shotgun had golden chains for hair that looked like snakes, hanging down shoulder-length. Dangling chains implanted in his scalp. A man with golden hair walked around like a god on earth. He hopped out of the trunk and came up to me, punting the mannequin's head down the road.

"Your goose is cooked," said Golden Hair.

"You must be Wes," I said.

"Elvis Presley had a Harley-Davidson made of fried chicken," he said.

"Probably didn't get very good gas mileage."

"Yes yes yes, the Martians call me Wes Wes Wes."

"What now?" I said.

"Time bomb, bok choy, bullet train," he said, his golden snakes dancing and hissing as he shook his head for effect. He pointed at Stink Phinger. "Can you get us inside this beguiling monastery?"

There. I had him. But I couldn't seem too eager.

"Why do we need to go inside?"

"Will you botch this sticky wicket?" he asked me, aiming the shotgun at my knee. "No way, Jose!"

"If you insist," I said.

"Bone broth, mustard gas, abstract expressionism," said Wes.

ᚹ

Wes led me inside with the shotgun in my back, the two arrowed men limping behind us. Wes told me to sit at the bar, and he knew how to control the distance between us. Unlike the ridiculous tweaker, who let the barrel be too close to me, Wes was out of harm's way, ten feet off.

The two wounded men clutched the arrows sticking from their legs, those little thespians.

Vikings, they were not.

They made their way behind the bar and poured well vodka on their wounds, and they both mewled like fussy newborns.

"This hurts," one said.

"The arrow or the vodka?"

"It's not an either-or situation."

I had to hold back laughter listening to them complain to each other.

"Should we pull them out?" one asked the other, getting ready to rip his arrow.

The other went wide-eyed. And stayed that way. Like a gambler waiting to see if he was gonna strike it rich or go broke.

"Wide eyes! That's all you have to add to the conversation?" his friend said. "Does that seem like enough at a time like this? I'd like a verbal response."

"These are unchartered waters," the other said.

"I'm at a crossroads here, man, and you're not weighing in. How do you think that feels to me?"

His friend thought for a minute, then said, "I've seen in movies where, once the knife or whatever that's been jammed into you gets yanked out, that's when the blood really starts gushing. We should learn from the mistakes of others."

"But movies aren't real."

"Some are."

"Documentaries. True crime. *Jackass*," Wes said. Then he spoke to me. "What would you recommend doing?"

"I hope they bleed out."

The wounded man who'd been skeptical of removing the arrows pointed and nodded at me. "Right. Exactly. I'm leaving mine in."

"Don't listen to him," the other arrowed man said. "He's the dick who did this to us."

"'Silent Night,' let the big boys talk," Wes ordered, then to himself: "Silent treatment, in treatment, trick or treatment."

Wes wasn't physically imposing. Five feet eight on a day wearing new boots. But all them chains anchored to his scalp, they sent a simple message: *If I've brought this much agony into my own life, what almighty spite do you think I could wield in yours?*

"Sexy singles in your area," Wes said to me. "Act now and receive a free parachute."

"Do you talk like this when the drugs wear off?"

"I never let the drugs wear off."

"You must," I said, "because the emails you sent Amy sounded pretty normal."

"I'm glad to hear they were convincing stories," he said. "Bestseller. Pulitzer. Pubic lice."

As much as I hated how he talked, in a way, it reminded me of the hectic noise of my own thoughts. Sometimes it sounded like I had a little Wes in my head.

He couldn't stand still. Jewelry jangling as he paced and raved. Gold snakes hissing from his head. "I'm claiming this as my own," he said. "Manifest destiny. Squatter's rights. Barbie's Dreamhouse."

"Claiming what?"

"I got the idea from your email," he said. "Thanks for making it all come true, trophy wife."

I loved his golden look, frankly. He looked like madness.

A proper enemy from an old Norse myth.

Maybe we were living a new legend.

And his madness incited some of my own—because I saw a worthy adversary, because I saw combat. It was wunjo. There was a new part of me that only wanted a Whole Foods life, sure, but there was this animal in me, too, and when I let that wildness and the fang take over, I could see molecules, could talk to nerve endings. I smelled the moon like it was a blooming flower.

Joy!

That was what I felt.

And Wes's frantic sermon chirped on—it was like he could hear my thoughts and tried to one-up me; it was like my brain noise and his spoken words were dueling, improvising musicians, trading licks and bars, turning the whole empty club hot.

"Knock on wood, knock you down, knock you up," said Wes, pacing as he talked, shaking his head, gold chains clashing, hissing his Medusa music. "So this is all mine now, and we never need to see each other again. You and Amy are old news, spoiled milk, moldy bagels."

Hearing him talk was like listening to lightning. He believed in his bones every flash of bent language he spoke. Conviction—that drug.

He said to me, "You'll convince Amy to sell me the club for twenty bucks, buyer's market, Bing Crosby, antifreeze."

"I won't," I said, "because fuck you."

"Oh, you wouldn't be doing it for me," he said. "Greenhouse gases. Zeus. Bikram Yoga. You'd do it for you."

"Do you always talk like a fortune cookie is having a stroke?" I asked.

He let the snakes hiss as he marched to where the arrowed guys were weighing their options. Wes eyeballed me, made sure there was enough space, and he set the shotgun down by the cash register behind the bar. Then he reached down for each of the arrows, and both men knew better than to buck.

Wes said to them, "Yahtzee, narwhal, claw hammer," and at the same time, he ripped the arrows out of both of their thighs. The men did everything they could to control their reactions. They knew what Wes was capable of, and despite some tears, they were as stoic as could be. Now Wes was holding both bloody arrows, and he did a little routine with them behind the bar, like a deranged baton twirler, sending them up into the air and catching them.

Wes said, "I heard that you took a finger from my friend Dusty. He said I shouldn't worry about it, but what can I say: I'm a worrywart! Driveshaft, Nintendo. So I get the club, or I cut off one of your fingers. Hard to play guitar without the index finger of your fret hand, huh?"

I was a person and he was a person, and you were there, too, watching the golden serpents shimmy on his scalp, and I wasn't scared in the slightest—I hope you weren't scared, too—because this was what I'd wanted all along. You didn't forget about the surprise, right? You remembered the thing I had Amy do, yeah? You remembered that I had something up my sleeve.

"How many bands have you robbed?" I asked Wes.

"I'm going to take your middle finger," he said. "You'll never give another bird. A sperm hits an egg. I'm going to Disney World!"

I motioned to the empty stage. "That's where the bands were supposed to play, right up until you robbed them."

I didn't need to get the shotgun back behind the bar. I just needed to block his route, just needed to make sure Wes didn't get the weapon before reinforcements barreled in.

"*Now!*" I said, launching myself over the bar, pushing the arrowless men out of my way, making sure Wes couldn't protect himself. Because this was when they all entered through the stage from the door in back of it, this was when they ran over the stage, jumped off it, and sprinted toward Wes. Their screams were a battle cry, they were wolves, each band that Wes had stolen from; forty or fifty heads poured into the room, a belligerent platoon, and they were ready for a good old-fashioned stomp.

Where the boots did the talking.

They gave Wes the ol' Jello Biafra special.

All these wonderful barbarians ready to take their hacks at the man who stole their gear. They were like pagans running through the castle of some Christian, somebody who wouldn't keep their religion to themselves, thank you very much, stop hocking your god, telling us how to live, and we weren't going to stand for it anymore, no, we weren't going to allow this, and we kicked down the door, and we raged through the halls, to the throne room, where this Christian hid behind a Bible, and we peeled the book from his hands and we ripped it in half, ate its pages—

They pulled Wes over the bar, to the floor; they pulled him across the floor, to the stage, planting him on it, dead center. They circled him. He was up there with them, and they were up there with him, and they were handing him his ass, and I wanted to contact the Academy to nominate this in the category of Best Revenge Stomp.

A glass bird landed on my shoulder and whispered guidance.

Of course!

It was the wisdom of the ancestors burping from the bird's beak. Funny, I didn't see him fly away, but he wasn't on my shoulder any longer, but it didn't matter, with the answer right on my lips. I mounted the stage, fought through the crush, picked Wes up.

He was bashed. Busted nose for sure. One of his arms hung straight down from the socket. He couldn't put weight on his leg. I said to the bands, "You've put a beating on this man you can be proud of. He'll be pissing blood all week. But he's had enough."

A couple of guys wanted to squawk at me about severing their revenge, but I warned them with my one eye: "Who thinks I'm kidding and who knows I'm not?" I asked.

"We know you're not," one said, "because you bit off Dusty's finger."

"How did you hear about that?"

"It's the kind of news that makes the rounds," he said.

"Well, I don't want to bite anybody else."

They quieted right up.

"You were all cheated out of thousands of dollars of gear," I said to them, and they nodded and shrugged, yup, that was right.

"Okay, so let's get you reimbursed," I said, turning my attention to Wes, asking him, "How many karats are those chains?"

"Twenty-four, car horn, chicken and waffles," he said.

"And how many of them are on your head?"

"Fifty-two. That's how old my old man was when he died, cue the topless dancer, tragic backstory, chutney."

I couldn't listen to his amphetamine poetry right now. I was in the middle of something way out of my comfort zone: trying to do arithmetic.

I made a face like someone doing math in his head.

Then I made the face of someone failing at that.

Then I made the face of someone quitting the equation altogether in shame.

Now I was back addressing the bands: "That should put each chain at about two thousand apiece multiplied by fifty-two, and that equals something pretty fucking high. Divide them up evenly. It won't cover everything, but it's payment. Plus, it will really fucking hurt."

And I took a step back. Watched them pluck his golden chains like they were stiff, wealthy feathers.

# 16

ONCE HAD A DREAM that was a horrible puzzle, and it started like this: a woman's face.

It was either my mother or my aunt.

I couldn't tell.

Whoever she was, she was a ghost. I knew that because it was what the woman said to me: "I'm a ghost."

"Are you my mother or my aunt?" I asked, and she said, "I'm both," and I said, "What do I call you?" and she said, "Freya and Frigg," and I asked, "Why are you here, Freya and Frigg?" and she said, "I am here to joyously haunt you."

Isn't that maybe the most beautiful thing you could ever say to somebody you love? *I am here to joyously haunt you!* It was perfect for us, because we were all shambling ghosts, trustworthy schizophrenics, flamboyant thieves, love-starved poets, snow-blind astronomers, greed weasels, mean chieftains twisted on vision mead and arguing with arrogant hallucinations—

*I am here to joyously haunt you!*

I'd never had a dream so inspiring, and I awoke renewed and elated, and I could hear those magic words working in me, I even sang them in the shower to a tune of my own invention, feeling that perhaps, just maybe, there was a path for me to follow to a rewarding future, even if no one had ever given me a map to get there. But soon I realized that if it was all a dream, no one was here to joyously haunt me, no one cared enough to do so, in fact the mere idea that anybody would ever love me enough was laughable. It was impossible to love me because you fell off a bar, or cut your throat, or got off the bus, and if people could love me, why were they always vanishing?

Here was a bad idea: turn a grieving Viking boy into a junkie.

That was the kind of thinking that set people up for success!

A grieving Viking junkie boy was a wolf with a heart of freezing iron. The Upper Haight was where I hunted. The Panhandle.

It was at that point in my life I really started to see the glass birds.

They began chattering once I finished the stash of morphine lollipops, and my body turned into a swamp, humid and burping. The birds were with me when I was awake and when I tried to sleep, and the birds weren't taking no for an answer. They needed lollipops. My head turned into a horrid Christian church, the birds ringing through me like pipes on a possessed organ.

I had a crap job stocking shelves at Walgreens, barely made enough to cover rent at Mom Jon's, and I didn't see another way to get more morphine, so what if I pulled a smash and grab?

Victimless crime.

And so what if I pulled a few smash and grabs?

They probably had insurance.

And so what if I pulled fifty smash and grabs?

A hundred?

And so what if one time, I'd put a tire iron through a window, and a man yelled, "Get away from my car!" and he approached me stupidly, and I tripped him and I was on top of him and I hit him only one time and I took his wallet and I took his watch and I took his laptop and I took his headphones and I took everything I could—and so what if I ran off with all my treasures?

It was the first time the birds gave their beaks a break, had a glass of water, let their lungs rest, and so what if I kept running away from the bloodied man, and there was so much adrenaline in my body, I was war high—sure, smash and grabs were keeping me in steady supply, but they didn't offer this other release—and I wanted to drop into an animal crawl, and if it wouldn't have made it impossible to tote all my rewards, I would've done just that, would've howled, would've let my fangs go wild.

And there were other smash and grabs because they were easy and safe.

But soon, my appetite for fight got the better of me.

I always came home thrashed. Broken nose or jaw or orbital or ribs or wrist, hands, fingers. A separated shoulder. But these were all worth it as I marauded the Haight, taking on all comers, often fighting more than one man at once.

Mom Jon was worried at first, then inconvenienced, then furious. "I've lost too many friends to the streets," she said. "Don't do it. Please."

But I didn't know how to stop. It had magic in it, the anger, and it filled me with such a single-minded purpose I was freed of all other troubles. Yes, in war, my heart was peaceful as a frozen lake.

I didn't stop fighting, so Mom Jon threw me out. I did ask her a favor on my way. It was getting to the point where I couldn't be trusted with the Tele. I'd hock it to score—and the idea of trading Keith Richards's and Tron's and my happy monster for drug money was too much.

"Will you please keep my guitar for me?" I said to Mom Jon.

"Why?"

"I'll lose it."

"But what if I don't see you again?"

"You will. I promise."

"I'm going to hold you to that," she said.

"Okay."

"Do you know why I'll keep the guitar for you, even though you're driving me absolutely crazy right now?"

"Why?"

"Because if I see you again, that might mean you've turned it around," she said.

"That's the plan."

"Come back for it."

"I will."

"In one piece."

"I'll try."

"One! Piece!" she said.

"Okay," I said, lying, laughing, and we hugged.

Once Mom Jon kicked me out, I cycled through punk houses in the Sunset, SoMa, the Mission—finally headed to the East Bay to the warehouse scene of West Oakland. Finally headed to that night that every junkie got to. The night that every sin committed decided to come back and get even.

I could tell you that I didn't mean to do it, and that was the truth. Older you got, though, the truth was another false god. Once the truth traveled into our feeling factories, it had as much shape as a plastic bag in a hurricane.

This man and I were having a fight, and fights were always right on the edge of somebody dying; we all knew the risks. Fighting was trying to solve a real-time puzzle. Whoever got the answer got the win.

I had all that glima training, all those matches.

I had all that time wrestling with the bear.

I had the hours hunting like a wolf in the Norwegian wilderness.

Even now, if I inhaled deeply, I could conjure the pine smell of those forests. You could put soil samples in my hand from dirt all over the world, and I'd be able to tell by feel the one from my father's land.

The man came at me with a clumsy attack, and I angled out and tripped his front foot, throwing off his balance, and I shoved him in the back, thinking he'd simply fall and I'd be on top of him, finish him with elbows to the face—but he staggered two steps first, right toward the car, and when he finally fell, his momentum carried his face straight into the front panel, snapping his neck too far back, so he looked straight up at the sky. He was dead.

I wanted more than anything to see him move, tried to convince myself: Maybe he looked to the sky because he was a stargazer.

But he was dead.

Or maybe he simply had his head in the clouds.

But he was dead.

Or he was praying, tilting his chin up so mightily so that his syllables traveled straight to the heavens, making sure none of his words got misconstrued. He hated being misquoted by the gods.

The last one seemed the most plausible, so that was what I went with: prayer. He was deep in a desperate plea, and who was I to interrupt his solo to the divine?

I didn't know this then, but I would spend time around the Christian god once I fell into the chomping maw of Quentin. I would spend hours doing something I never could've imagined, hoisting the Christian Bible, that book of aggression, ego, demolition—the written tonic they tried to pour over the whole world to make us swallow their septic beliefs. I wasn't reading their lies, of course, but since California had taken weights out of prisons in the late '90s, I had to fill my laundry bag with Bibles to make my own gym, doing reps with the laundry bag, up and down, hundreds every day.

Curls, shoulder presses, squats, ab work, bench.

Lifting the book I hated.

Holding the Bibles high—this thing that I despised, that took so much from my people.

Every time I wanted to quit the workout, to set that bundle of books down, muscles shaking, seizing, I only had to think about what I was holding—and there was no way I was gonna let myself be bested by a laundry bag of Bibles.

But remember, I didn't know anything about that standing next to this dead man.

Maybe this was the moment right before his prayer ended, and once it was done, he'd stand to full height, smile at me, and say, *Life is too short for us to behave like cavemen. Instead let's dance with pretty women, let's dance with ugly women, let's dance with anybody with suffering in their hearts—because at the end of our lives, all we want is one more minute here, in this confusing slop.*

And I stood there because, maybe, he was about to say all that.

And I waited to be taken to Niflheim—that gnawing world of the dead.

And I said to nobody because I was all alone, "I am here to joyously haunt you."

Half an hour after they'd yanked the fifty-two chains from Wes's scalp, leaving little craters all over his head like a blubbering moon, his body was busted.

Trick was with me now.

Wes was finally coming back to consciousness, taking in his surroundings. Then he looked at me, laughed, and understood immediately that here, I was the shot caller, the guard, the warden, and the governor who'd never even heard of pardons. I was the parole board. I was his piss tests, his PO, his ankle bracelet, his halfway house, his scabies, itching all night. I was his low-wage future, his low-watt faith, his next offense. I was the judge busting him back to the pen, where I was the shot caller, the guard, the warden, and—wait, haven't we done this already?

My dad might have been right when he said Vikings couldn't bear cages. I couldn't. There wasn't a second inside that I didn't hate it, but doing time was just a little bit better than slicing my own throat.

I thought about it.

Of course.

I thought about Tron's suicide most days before I was locked up, so it was only natural to brandish that fetish on myself.

There were voices, loud voices—and they spoke only in the middle of the night. *Valhalla,* they said, *is waiting. Quentin is a battlefield. Die and find peace.*

It wasn't a big deal to die in there. Nobody cared. You were a number on a shirt. Math and no more. It wasn't a crime to kill a number.

I despised Wes, but I didn't want him to be put in a cage. No, I had something much better in mind.

"I am going to strip you naked, drive you to some hellhole, and you'll get out with nothing but the hair on your balls, and you'll watch me drive off, and you'll never come back to the bay."

"Kamikaze, Beelzebub, Captain Beefheart," he said. "I haven't sold all the gear yet. What if I tell you where what's left is?"

"Where?"

"My storage locker. Psylocibin. Hitler mustache. I can give you the address, if you can cure my scurvy and apocalypse flu." He began shouting the addy over and over. Trick wrote it on the back of her hand in Sharpie. "Are you still going to leave me in a hellhole?" he asked.

"Of course I am," I said.

"Good soldier, designated driver, hedge fund leper, bombardier."

"The quicker we get him in the trunk the better," Trick said to me.

"Agreed."

"I'll go with you," she said.

"You don't have to."

"I want to. Because as soon as we get rid of his sorry ass, we're going to check into a motel."

# 17

ONCE WES WAS LOADED UP in the trunk, I left Trick in the car to guard him so I could say goodbye to Jesse and Amy. I walked to her office in the back of Stink Phinger. I fished the deed to her club from my pocket and handed it back to her. She sat at her desk and looked at it in her palm like it was a dead fish.

"Why is it wet?" she asked.

"Remember? I swam from your boat to shore?"

"Right. I've got a hair dryer in my desk. It gives me a project while Jesse entertains me with his performance-vomit routine."

Jesse was unconscious on the small couch, in the fetal position, kicking his legs like a slumbering, haunted dog. The upside-down umbrella had filled with retched broth.

Amy was still looking at the wet deed in her hand, considering something.

Suddenly, a worry expanded in my guts: "I hope you don't burn this place, too," I said to her. "I hope you decide to stay in business and run it right."

"I'm staying in business, for sure," she said. "I'll crash at Jesse's and help him. He gets a free nurse and I get a place to stay until I sort this all out. I need to think. But I'm staying in business. That's a promise."

"Who are you making that promise to?" I said.

Amy studied me for a beat. "You should run the club with me," she said.

"I am recently unemployed."

"I did hear something about that."

"I'm going on tour for a couple weeks."

"So after tour," she said, "let's make some changes around here."

ᚠ

You're a person who has this story sloshing in your mind's eye, that sick Chihuahua, that bereaved computer, that knockoff crematorium, that graffitied body bag, that mad dirge, that worm dessert, that battle dog, that mildewed cathedral, that shell-shocked sarcophagus, that time-share cemetery, that silver-tongued tick, that deathbed chain saw, that deathbed kiss, Odin calling you home for mead and hearsay—

Wait.

Was that me thinking, or Wes talking?

I was driving the Reliant forged during the American Revolution. Trick Wilma was next to me. Wes was in the trunk, and now he was screaming, "I've given many Costa Ricans venereal diseases!"

He laughed and showed no signs of abating. He was naked back there. He jostled around the trunk like forgotten groceries.

Groceries that could talk.

Groceries that could go, "I'm trying to send a dick pic to the head ventriloquist of Jupiter."

"Shut the fuck up!" Trick said.

"You don't have to eat all the cheese, Marilyn," said Wes.

Maybe he had his own glass birds keeping him company. Or he was just crazy. As we sped up 80 toward Tahoe, Wes lived in darkness, in a bumping, speeding metal womb. Trick and I listened to one of my favorite records, *The Streets of San Francisco*. We held hands and decided to crank the music to drown out any slam poetry from Wes.

We had gotten good news. An hour back, Got Jokes called to say that about half the bands' gear was at that warehouse. The rest of it had been sold. They divvied up the gold chains to favor the gearless.

Now, Trick pointed to a bend in the road. "Right up here," she said as we bumped down some hillbilly lane. "He's thirty miles from civilization. That's good enough."

I stopped the car. The air smelled clean and like redwood, not the wastewater oxygen we were used to.

Trees, dirt, insects, snakes, animals.

And us.

"What now?" Trick asked me. "Do we . . . pop the trunk and that's it?"

Seemed as good an idea as any, so I opened it from the driver's seat, pulling a little lever, releasing Wes. He didn't get out at first, then he struggled to his feet. He came around to the window, standing there naked and looking at us. I was still adjusting to seeing him without the golden snakes dangling from his scalp. His head was disgusting now, a garden of open scabs.

"What happened to my foot?" he said, referencing the nail I had pounded in while he was unconscious.

Now, listen, hear me out . . .

Why did I do that? Well, it happened as I was putting him in the trunk and thought, *The bands have had their day in court with Wes, plucking those gold chains from his dome—but Jesse hasn't gotten any justice.* He hadn't been able to lift himself out of the withdrawal quicksand to participate, and so I would act as his proxy. With his new nail, Wes would slither through mud, and the infection in his wound would be his only companion.

So I told him a half-truth: "You stepped on a nail."

Technically, not untrue.

"Huh," he said, "I don't remember."

"That's because he's lying," Trick said.

"Hey," I said to her, "let me enjoy this."

"The sooner we're done here, the sooner we're at the motel," she said. "You'll enjoy that more."

"It definitely feels like there's a nail in my foot," Wes said.

"I wasn't lying about that part," I said.

"I see," Wes said. "You lied about *how* it got there."

"Yeah, I nailed it in with a hammer."

"Ouch."

"You're not talking like a crystal meth jack-in-the-box anymore," I said to him.

"It doesn't feel like the time," he said.

"I actually like it," I said. "I think how you talk. It makes me won—"

"Oh, wow, I'm just realizing that I am nude," he said. "And where are we?"

"We're releasing you back into the wild," I said.

"Why?"

"Because I promised myself that I wouldn't kill you."

He stood there a minute, looking down at his naked body, then examined the bottom of the nailed foot by standing flamingo style. He really did look like a demented plucked bird, with those bright red polka dots on his head, weeping, glistening Christmas ornaments.

Speaking of birds, this was the moment I heard them, up here in the forest. I couldn't see the glass birds, but it was them. I would know their caws anywhere, just like how a mother could hear ten babies cry and knew which was hers.

"Hey, do you hear those birds?" Wes asked.

Wait.

He could hear the birds?

Nobody but me could ever see or hear them, since Tron had been gone.

In that instant, time lost its math.

We'd traveled inside someone's fever.

Wes said it again: "Hey, do you hear those birds?"

"Of course," I said, big gusts of wunjo billowing through me. "I'm surprised you can."

"Are they your personal birds?" Wes said.

"Most likely. That's my best guess."

"And we're the only two who can hear them?"

"I don't know."

"I can hear them," he said, "but I don't understand what they're saying. But you can, right? They make sense to you?"

"They're wondering where you're gonna walk to."

Wes thought for a minute.

We heard the cranky, idling engine of the Reliant. We heard the nervous energy between us. We heard one redwood tell another that it was hogging all the water.

"Will you take all the birds with you when you go," Wes asked, "or will any of them stay with me?"

"I don't tell them what to do."

"I bet they like that about you," he said. "It feels like I'm supposed to say something important. But I don't believe that anything is important. I haven't ever met one thing that matters in my whole life. That was how I ended up with so many holes in my head. And without any speed on me, I'm going to withdraw out here. I'm going to roll on the ground like a dying dog. I'll scream like I'm giving birth. So it doesn't seem like there's much else to say," and then he slipped back into his madhouse character: "But maybe I'll walk to West Virginia. Normally, I'd take my submarine, but I left the keys in my chamber pot."

"You're going to have a long night. Enjoy the withdrawal and tetanus."

I reached into a box in the back seat, retrieved the reflective paint. I threw it to Wes.

"What's this for?" he said.

"Reflective paint. Put it all over your body, you peacock."

He chuckled as he painted his whole naked body the color of a lightning bolt. Then he dug his fingers into the holes on his head, like he was a bowling ball. Quickly, he took on the magnetism of a street preacher, and Trick and I were the only lucky humans who had tickets to the show.

There he stood, this nude golden mad poet with his fingers in his head. He took his time, took in the wilderness of the theater. Yes, he really did look like he'd been struck by lightning, absolutely elated to be alive, we could feel watts of charisma, and then, with one big breath, the biggest I'd ever seen someone take, he boomed: "Bongos. Self-righteous labia. Empathy assault rifle. Willy Wonka diabetes. Catacombs. Flamenco guitar. Don't let the bedbugs bite. Motor oil wet nurse. Roaring Twenties. Stray cat. Whooping cough. Doomsday clock. Yoga mat. Garden gloves. Gasp. Feelings. Kudos. Pruno. Popsicles. Mad Hatter. Kangaroo court. Tote the rock. C'est la vie."

By this point in his frantic sermon, his face was rhubarb red, and he barely had enough air to eke out the remaining landslide of words—but he was going to make it—the show, my friends, was gonna go on, hell yes, he would see to that—

"Tube socks. Slingshot. Dime bag. Mouthwash. Jazz hands. Ouija board. Tongs. Side effects include Georgia O'Keeffe. Hit dogs holler. Laryngitis casserole. Existential sweatpants. Lava lamp. Laughing gas. Gonads. Gesundheit!"

He stopped, our lunatic conductor, out of breath, spent. It might have been the middle of the night in the middle of the forest, but he stood basking in the UV rays of the limelight. Then I decided to give him one final little break, clapping for his greasy soliloquy, sitting right there in the Reliant, applauding.

For the record, Trick did not clap.

"Party foul, tattletale, welfare check," Wes said.

"Anything else you'd like to add before this is over?" I asked Trick.

"It's motel time," she said.

We kissed, and for a minute we forgot that Wes stood there, golden and naked with a nail in his foot. He must've gotten tired of waiting for us because he coughed to regain our attention.

"I guess I'll see myself out, swan song, coup de grâce, blah blah blah," he said, holding one arm up in adulation and exiting the stage by limping into the trees.

P

We found a motel on our drive back, received a little key that was tied to a big spoon so people didn't keep stealing it, and we opened our door and she walked in and I followed to a tiny bathroom, and we began taking our clothes off, began seeing each other, all of us, head to toe—and we climbed into the shower, and we stood in our birthday suits, and we kissed, and our bodies touched, and her name was Wil and mine was Saint, and this was the kind of moment that killed you with its simplicity: You were nothing but self-destructive desire—a desire that you'd do anything to quench.

Then she told me that I was still wearing one article of clothing, but I had nothing on. I was showing her everything.

"Your eye patch," she said. "I want you to take it off."

Did it make you wonder how I lost it, every time my eye came up? Going into Quentin, I'd known the thousand reasons I could be killed. A friend of mine got murdered for playing checkers with the wrong man, and if checkers could get you killed . . .

When you were new, one of the gangs might make you hide weapons in your cell for them, which added years to your sentence if you were busted with contraband. Most newbies bent the knee. You had no choice, not really. If they wanted you dead, they had the numbers.

I told you earlier that someone lanced my eye, and that was true. I just didn't tell you that man was me. Maybe during our next saga I will be strong enough to tell you that story—but right now, those were impossible lyrics for me to sing.

Right now, all I could do was stand in this shower, in this motel, with Wil. We were two wolves, and she wanted to see everything.

"Okay," I said, reaching for the eye patch, "here we go."

# WHOLE FOODS HALLUCINATION

OVER THE SPEAKERS, Green Day played in Whole Foods. Billie was behind his regular register.

"I hear your gig was great," said Billie.

"It was—and we picked up a tour."

"Supporting Jawbreaker?"

"I'm a huge fan of theirs," I said.

"Did you really bite off your friend's finger?!"

"He deserved it."

"If you say so."

"It was the kind of day where I broke someone's wrist early on and somehow knew worse violence barreled right at me."

"So what brought you by the store today?" Billie asked. "Snacks for the first leg of the tour?"

"Actually—and I don't mean to put you on the spot—but, uh, I was wondering: Are you guys hiring here? I recently needed to quit my job as a cocaine dealer's right-hand man. I'm qualified to do little else but play guitar and fight people."

"You? Want to work? At Whole Foods?"

"I do."

"I can put in a word with my manager," Billie said.

"That's very nice of you. You're nice."

"You know, Saint, the first time we met? I didn't think you liked me very much."

"Huh?" I said, flabbergasted by such an accusation.

"You thought I was a sellout or something," he said.

"That's not true."

"Come clean, man."

"You'll never be my favorite band, but I like you," I said to him. "And if I'm being honest, I don't begrudge you your success. I want people to love my music the way they love yours."

Billie said, "Yeah, and I've never even heard one note from your band—and you need to fix that fast."

"We'll record."

"And gig out."

"As many as we can play."

"I was only busting your balls," Billie said. "Of course you can have a job here. Let me look under the desk. Gimme a second . . . Okay. Good. Here's one. An apron. Tie it on."

"Don't I fill out an application?"

"Don't worry about it."

"And I'm starting now?"

"Yes," he said, "you work here now."

"Right now?"

"If you want."

"Thanks, Billie. I appreciate it. If you'll take a chance on me, I'll work to prove to you that I am, in fact, Whole Foods material."

"I can see you're trying," he said, "and I want to help."

"I always want to help people, too," I said, "and sometimes it gets me in trouble. I don't always help the right way."

"People like us," Billie said, "we like life with a little bit of drama."

"Billie, your drama got you world famous. My drama got me locked up."

"It's not my fault that I picked a better drama than you," said Billie.

# EPILOGUE
## CODEX REGIUS

**I HELD A RAZOR NEAR DUSTY.** He looked nervous.

It was, technically, the next day, but it was earlier in the morning than when Got Jokes had knocked yesterday. So all this magic, technically, was just one day in my life.

To recap: Dusty looked nervous because I held a razor near him.

We were in our studio at Sound Check. The gigantic stuffed teddy bear was still jammed in the wall. He sat on the couch—Dusty, I meant, not the bear—and I kneeled in front of him with the razor.

Which was near his face.

"Hold still," I said to Dusty.

"This is still."

"Stiller."

"The stillest—that's what I'm doing."

"If you even move an inch," I said.

"Just get it out of the way already."

"Any last requests?"

"Pay off my student loans."

"Most colleges don't offer a cocaine-dealing taxi driver degree."

"It's liberal arts," he said. "I know there's nothing I can say to change your mind about this. It's right in your eye. Your mind's made up."

"Anyone you want me to contact on your behalf after this is over?" I asked.

"I once fell in love with a surf champion with ten-foot legs. I only saw her on TV, and that was enough. Those long legs. I've loved her ever since."

"What should I tell her?"

"That I'm a good dancer. She would've liked that about me. We could've danced as the sun came up. Oh, and tell her I make a hell of a goat cheese omelet."

"I'll pass that along."

"So this has to happen," he said.

"You have to pay the price for what you did."

"I've lost my job, my future, my finger," he said. "Isn't that enough?"

I shook the razor playfully back and forth. "No, it's not."

"Okay," he said, "goodbye," and Dusty cinched his eyes shut, went blind to the horror of the moment—of seeing something that he couldn't bear witnessing.

Now, the razor moved, slowly, methodically, and—

I made a first stroke down his dustache.

Did I get ya?

Losing the dustache was his final penalty. Granted, it was a ceremonial one. We could all agree that biting off his finger was his real sentence.

If I had it to do over again, I definitely wouldn't have taken it, if you were asking me today.

Other days, I could argue both sides.

"This hurts," he said. "You're killing me, man."

I hacked another small shrub from his upper lip. And with one more slice from the razor, the dustache was no more.

He was officially de-dustached.

"Would you like to see the damage?" I asked.

"Of course not."

"You're never gonna look?"

"Not until it grows back."

"Which can't be for a year."

"I know."

"Because that was the arrangement."

"I regret this already," he said.

It might not make sense to you why I'd forgive Dusty. I'd understand if that was your stance. But we'd had some proper adventures, and before that day, he'd always been nails when things needed to get bloody. And though our old band sounded like magnificent shit, I loved making music with him. You could ask anybody who played, who really played, and they'd ignore all kinds of bullshit and addictions and war if the songs were fists—ninety-second bullets of music.

The songs were all that mattered.

Punk rock was a wrecked guitar, bent and awful sounding, and it was the music of our peculiar kingdom.

I'd really trusted Dusty, and I believed it was possible to trust him again, though that would take time. He could regrow his dustache in a year's time, so we'd see what else returned, and yes, I realize how Whole fucking Foods that sounded.

"I'm bringing you back from the dead," I said to Dusty. "Like me. Like Jesse. Like Amy."

"They'd want me to have my dustache," he said.

ᛈ

I invited Trick and Got Jokes back into the practice room. I asked her to shut her eyes and extend an open palm. She smiled in anticipation. Then Dusty dropped the remnants of the dustache in her hand.

Immediately, she shot me the *what the fuck* face. "Was that your idea?" she said to me. "What's the matter with you?"

"Hold on," I said. "It's about to make sense."

"I don't want it to make sense. I just don't want a mustache—"

"Dustache," said Dusty.

"My hand has a no mustache policy," Trick said to me.

"Dustache," he said again.

The way this had worked out in my head was sweet and ended with Trick finding some romance in the gesture. She'd see it as an attempt to create the language of inside jokes. But what was in my head was not happening.

I tried to stay on script. "Say it," I said to Dusty.

"This pays my debt," he said to her. "Sorry, I was involved"—he glowered at me—"however indirectly, with what Wes did to your band."

She shot me another of those friendly faces and asked, "Why does he need to apologize to me?"

"That's what I said," said Dusty.

"Shut up," I said.

"He sold Wes's drugs," said Trick. "He wasn't involved in the band crap."

"That's what I said," said Dusty to me.

Trick puffed the dustache from her palm, and we all watched the hairs sashay and land on the ground. It had looked so good on his face.

"That made me very sad," Dusty said. "Like finding-out-there's-no-Santa sad."

"Not me," Trick said to him. "Whether or not you were involved with my gear getting stolen, I still think you're an asshole for not having Saint's back."

"I realize this isn't the best time," he said, "but if your band ever needs another musician—"

"I'm going to stop you right there," Got Jokes said. "Saint already took my job. So if anyone is ever in line to join, it's me."

That day—that one day in my life—it had started with the plainest thing, with a knock on my door, and from there, an adventure unfurled, a journey laced with danger and mystery, the day that I became Saint, a day of monsters and songs.

Þ

The Reliant had been loaded with our gear, and it was time for us to go, to ride the open ocean in our longship. We were in Sound Check's parking lot, ready to shove off.

"I'm so high my nose feels heavy," Got Jokes said to us. He lay across the back seat, seemed to have lost most of his bones. "Like a softball. Or a grenade."

"What's his deal?" I asked Trick.

"Too many edibles," she said.

"So he'll be stoned and stupid the whole way?" I said. "That's actually great news."

"This nose of mine—it's tuba heavy," said Got Jokes.

"Be quiet now," I said to him.

"I can do that," he said, then after a couple seconds, he said, "Did you hear that?"

"There was nothing to hear," I said.

"I couldn't tell if I was thinking or whispering. But if you didn't hear anything, I guess I was thinking," Got Jokes said.

"I seriously doubt that."

"I had to be thinking."

"Okay. Go back to thinking."

"Good advice," he said. "That sounds relaxing."

I fired up the Reliant, with its smashed windshield from Trick's rock storm, and now the ride had one improvement: Trick had surprised me with a dragon head hood ornament, making it a proper sailing vessel, warning everyone who witnessed us barreling toward their town that the Vikings were coming.

We were just about to set off, and I asked if we could make one quick stop on our way to tour. I wanted to say goodbye to Hild.

She was behind the counter when I came in. She said, "Are you like my dipshit boy from Detroit—or did you do the right thing?"

"That," I said, "is a complicated question."

"But you're here."

"I am."

"And it's over?"

"It is."

"And that badass girl?"

"She's right outside. We're leaving on a short tour. I wanted you to know that I'm all right—that I'm safe."

"Hey, Saint," Hild said to me. "Can I give you some advice in the form of a question?"

It sounded like something a parent might say—and I could see how grown children might resent such intrusions if they received them on the regular. But since I didn't, I had no idea how to feel anything except curiosity.

I said to her, "Please."

"We have two valves on our hearts," she said. "One lets in sunshine, the other lets in sewage. Which one are you gonna turn on?"

I hadn't expected her to say anything serious, and it took me a minute to understand what she was asking. Which valve would be thrown open to spill its flow?

It made me imagine an anatomical heart with two firehose veins, carrying their raw materials . . .

If you threw the wrong one open, you were going to have a sewage heart, pumping that sick stew to the rest of the body.

Or we could turn on the sunshine, and it could barrel into us like heated honey. And we could be warmed.

Making it a binary was bullshit, of course. In this life, it was never one or the other. Our hearts had that bare-knuckle battle day after day: the sewage or the sunlight.

Hild asked me this question at a moment of absolute joy. Trick and I were about to make music on our first tour. I was experiencing a kind of joy that felt dangerous. Dangerous in its optimism, which was its own drug.

And between you and me, I worried that Trick wouldn't want to live a Whole Foods life. I did meet her as she swung the sledgehammer. I watched this Valkyrie during that day and never saw her flinch once, which was electrifying, yes, but what if a Whole Foods existence didn't possess enough fire for her? If I had to choose between them, I knew myself well enough to know I'd abandon this quiet life and follow her to ruin.

Of course, there were no ways to know the answers, and since this was already a moment of dangerous wunjo, why not have another hit of it? Why not be dumb enough to believe we could pull it off? What was wrong with a delusion if it made you feel so high?

So, in that spirit, I stood up very straight, and I said to Hild, "I'm going to turn on the sunshine."

ᚦ

Tonight was the seventh show of the tour, and All the Fuss was getting ready to gig at El Corazón in Seattle. The opener had their gear scattered onstage, sound checking, and the drummer hit his kit, tom by tom, the speakers shaking like electric popcorn, so the soundman could get it right on the mixing board.

The tour had been the best week and a half of my life. Each night, I stood onstage hearing Trick growl, challenge these packed rooms to defy her commands, and no one knew how. She was a witch who made them drink henbane, and they were all stoned on her medicine, pinned eyes gleaming up at us.

And now, Trick, Got Jokes, and the unnamed drummer were sleeping on the club's floor over by the bar. Jawbreaker was outside resting in their much nicer wheels, while our Reliant with the dragon head hood ornament didn't have enough room to sleep.

I stood at the bar, waiting on a fake beer from the bartender. She wore a shirt that said DON'T STARE AT MY TITS.

Then I heard, from behind me, a man say, "Hey, I hear you're Saint? Saint the Terrifying?"

I turned to him. A gutter punk. Young. "Yeah, I'm Saint."

"Jesus, you're big."

"I am."

"Is it true—what they say happened?"

"What do they say?"

"About . . ." He leaned close to me and whispered, "That you bit off three of your old bandmate's fingers."

"It was only one."

"Still," he said, "one's pretty cool. And my band—we wrote—" and he blushed, looked away from me, shy like a child.

"You wrote what?" I asked.

"We, uh, it's—thing is, as soon as the guy told us—"

"Who was it?"

"Every band up and down the coast has heard the story."

"I didn't know that."

"We wrote a song about it."

"About me biting a finger off?"

"Would you like to hear our finger-biting song?" he said.

Trick walked up to us, yawning from her floor nap. "Hear your what?" she asked him.

The guy pointed at his crew up onstage, getting ready to sound check. "That's my band. We wrote a song about Saint the Terrifying."

She looked at me like he'd asked for driving directions to the bottom of the ocean.

"The chewed-off finger," I said to her, making some eating noises.

"You wrote a song about fingers," she said to him.

"I mean, *everyone* is talking about that," he said.

"No one has ever written a song about me," I said.

"Enough foreplay," said Trick to him. "Play the goddamn track."

He put his hands up in surrender and scurried toward the stage, nabbed his guitar, and they kicked into the song, a snarling riff, a sea monster, a gangster, a berserker, and Trick took my hand, yes, we held hands right there and listened to my song, and I was a person with a PORN STAR eye patch, and you were a person reading this myth, and how I wished you could hear this song, too . . .

Maybe it might be popular by the time you picked this up, maybe it could even play in Whole Foods someday, not that fame mattered to me, I just meant maybe you'd dig it, and the longer they played my song, I got hopped up on joy again—it could have a velocity, joy; it could speed you to your most embarrassing wish, humiliating only in how badly you wanted it to be your rescue, but I didn't need to go anywhere else, because this was all I wanted, this just-right joy, Trick Wilma's sweaty palm in mine, listening to something utterly unthinkable.

My father had been wrong about burning his book all those years. It was okay to leave something for the future. It was okay to turn into a scribble on a cave wall, a sacred text, a secret whispered around a fire. It was okay if you were something to be discovered long after you were gone, because we needed to pass on our stories, one confused human to another.

Trick leaned over, kissed me on the neck, screamed in my ear: "What do you think of your song?"

What did I think?

This was Valhalla.

This was home.

I couldn't answer her yet. I wasn't trying to be rude. Soon. That was a promise. But for now, I was busy inside this song, and I could only shut my eye and listen.

I was gonna stay here as long as I could.

I wanted to live in this song and never pay rent.

And while we're on the subject of illegal squats, thanks for letting me live in your head, thanks for listening, you light elf—and if you don't know what a light elf is, look it up, I'm giving you a compliment.

If I'm being honest, I've liked my time in your mind, though it sounds like you've got glass birds of your own up here in this roach motel, this bridezilla, this handicapped parking space, this chop shop time machine, this truffle pig hunting the delicacy of trauma—

And you've done a good job hiding it, and I could barely spot it way in the back of your brain, but it was there, abandoned, buried under the body weight of your ghosts—

your joy,

and your joy,

and your joy—